I0603400

ABOUT THE AUTHOR

Kellie Cox is an Australian writer indulging her love of fiction and prose. With qualifications in psychology, she relishes writing about the human condition and the vulnerability of the psyche. A therapist, clinical trainer, creative coach and conservationist, she enjoys a dream life on the beautiful Gold Coast.

Wanting to see a change in the narrative of gender roles in storytelling, Kellie has created her publishing and production enterprise, Strong Female Protagonists and encourages others to write and produce work that challenges our preconceived notions of societal values.

Most days Kellie can be found working with artists in the creative industries or writing her novels. When not writing, Kellie will likely be saturating her social media accounts with photos of her adorable dogs.

Follow Kellie on social media as KellieCoxWriter and KellieMCox.

www.kelliemcox.com
www.strongfemaleprotagonists.com

WRITTEN BY KELLIE M COX

Fiction
Murderous Intent (2019)
The Last First Kiss (2020)
The List (2020)
The Reef (2020)

Short Stories
Death by Trident (2018)
Short Yarns for Big Imaginations, GCWA.

THE REEF

Book Two

KELLIE M COX

Strong Female Protagonists

THE REEF

This book is a work of fiction. Names, characters, places and incidents are the product of the author's imagination or are used fictitiously. Any resemblance to actual events, or persons, living or dead, is entirely coincidental.

Copyright © 2020 Kellie M Cox

The moral right of the author has been asserted. All rights reserved. No part of this book may be reproduced or transmitted by any person or entity, including internet search engines or retailers, in any form or by any means, electronic, mechanical including photocopying (except under the statutory exceptions provisions of the Australian Copyright Act 1968), recording, scanning or by any information storage and retrieval system without the prior written permission of Kellie M Cox and Strong Female Protagonists Publishing.

Published by Kellie M Cox
and

 Strong Female Protagonists

www.KellieMCox.com
www.StrongFemaleProtagonists.com

ISBN 978 0 6484767 4 0 (paperback)
ISBN 978 0 6484767 5 7 (ebook)
Author - Kellie M Cox
Cover Photo – Georgina Winters
Cover Design - Blair Renwick
Logo and Website Design – Connor Renwick

DEDICATION

And to my beautiful mother, who fell in love with this story and has waited years for it to be published. Thank you for your endless encouragement to write.

And

To everyone, wondering if the person in your life is indeed your very own soul mate. May you too have that magical moment when they do something so special that your tears well and your throat gets caught and you know finally and with absolute certainty that they are The One!

Hope you enjoy the read!

ONE

THE MESSAGE

He watched his friends ascend the staircase to the third floor. For a moment, he felt alone, more alone than he had remembered feeling for years. Once again, he turned his attention to the envelope in his hand. Willing his eyes to read through the paper to spare him the pain of ripping open the seal.

He needed to find somewhere quiet to read the letter. He headed toward the kitchen, quickly exiting through the back door and onto the terrace. He made his way to the daybed and perched himself on the edge.

He placed his spare hand on the plump cushion feeling the fabric beneath his palm, remembering back to the night he professed his love to Kasie. His thoughts turned to Kasie but his eyes closed to shut out the pain of her. He dared not try to imagine where she was right now. He didn't want to visualise her anywhere but beside him. He looked at the envelope again.

Sensing that he needed to get it read quickly, he tore open the envelope and unfolded the crisp, clean white stationery in front of him. He closed his eyes once more, took in a deep breath, held it for just a moment and let the breath move through his lips into the chilly night air. He held the note between his two hands, moved his eyes to the words and began to read;

I will never forgive myself for doing this to you.
I need to go home. Please don't follow me. I am so sorry for hurting you like this. Please forgive me.

I will always love you.
Kasie

He let out a wail that could be heard from the bedroom above.

* * *

Marco, having already placed Dee gently under the covers of her bed made his way to the window to look down and see his best friend, slumped over, his head in his hand. The letter now removed from the envelope in his other hand. He wanted to go to him, to help him through this unbearable moment in time, but he knew that Dee needed him too and her current emotional state was precarious.

Marco stood at the window a moment longer. He watched as his friend, as if not believing what he had first read lifted his head from his hand to re-read the words before him again.

* * *

He read every word once more, the pain on second reading somehow magically accumulating in strength to create a huge chasm where his heart once was.

He slowly devoured the last few words, *I will always love you.* The only words he chose to believe from the heartbreaking message. He read on and noticed for the first time, something that his anguish allowed him to overlook on his first reading;

P.S. Always remember… home is where the heart is.

* * *

The sun finally rose on what felt the longest night of their lives. It was a restless and painful night for the three. Unable to sleep, he stayed in his office searching through photos, scanning through notes and research documents trying to make sense of the mystery. Kasie had been gone for over twelve hours now, long enough to be far away from Coral Cove and far away from the fairytale life that he had wanted to provide for her.

Marco, who had remained in the upstairs bedroom managed to finally catch an hour or two sleep on the leather lounger overlooking the vast ocean that swept out beyond the mansion walls. He didn't want to leave Dee on her own. Unable to imagine the torment she had been through the previous night; he chose to be there when she woke. Having called on the nursing staff still on hand to care for Kasie, Dee had accepted from them a Valium in an attempt to calm her and help her get some rest.

It had worked and she managed to finally get some sleep in the early hours of the morning. As the sun began to shine through the bedroom window, warming the room in with its beams, Marco heard Dee stir and walked toward the bed and sat down beside her.

"Dee, how are you feeling?" he enquired gently.

"Has Kasie come back yet?" she pleaded hopefully, not yet fully awake.

"No, not yet," Marco regretfully replied. "But soon, I am sure we will all be seeing her again soon. Try to get some more rest."

"I can't," she argued with him.

"Come on Dee, we need you rested and strong to help find her, get some more sleep, please."

It didn't take much further convincing, with the Valium, the trauma and the exhaustion of the night before, Dee really couldn't muster the energy to move out of the bed and quickly fell back to sleep. Looking out at the sun rising above the ocean, Marco decided to leave Dee for a while to search the mansion for his best friend.

Within minutes he had found his boss, his best friend, slumped over his expansive wooden and leather desk, scanning documents and photos on his laptop.

"What are you looking for?" Marco enquired as he entered the room.

"Anything, anything at all," he explained.

Marco knowing his best friend as he did, knew there would be more calculated methods behind his search than what he was letting on.

"Could I read the note?" Marco asked him hesitantly.

His boss raised his eyes from the laptop, bloodshot from the lack of sleep. He had only ever seen his friend in this much pain once before. He recalled the car accident that took his mother and father, both young, both vibrant and both wonderful parents. He didn't know at the time how his friend would cope with the tragic and senseless loss of both of his parents at once. But here he was again. Battling this irrational and confusing disappearance of the only woman he had ever loved.

"She has left Marco. The note said she has returned home to Australia."

"Can I please read it?" Marco repeated his request for his grief-stricken friend.

Without a further word in reply, he handed Marco the note. Marco scanned the letter, not once, not twice, but three times, each time refusing to believe the words before him, written in her own handwriting.

"I don't understand. I just don't understand." He repeated his confusion as if hoping the repetition would make things clearer for him. "This just doesn't sound like her at all," Marco finally concluded.

"But it does, read it again, it sounds like what she would say if she were to do this face to face." His friend explained. "She talks of feeling sorry, of not wanting to hurt me. These are the words she would use."

"But she also says she will love you forever. What does that mean? This just doesn't feel right to me." Marco continued to remain doubtful of the words before him, even if his boss was determined to believe them.

The door to the office opened ever so gently as both men caught a glimpse of Kasie's best friend, Dee. Having arrived in Coral Cove from Australia just days earlier, she had sat by her friend's bed praying for her to wake up from her drug-induced coma. She was overjoyed to watch her friend begin to recover from the horrific attack on her life and even happier to watch as the love between her and the man she had dubbed Prince Charming began to blossom.

"I'm sorry to disturb you," she apologised as she entered the room.

"It's alright, how are you feeling?" Marco enquired. "I thought you were getting some more sleep."

"I can't rest anymore. I was hoping that I could read the note from Kasie." Dee looked down at the handwritten note in Marco's hand. "Is that it?" she asked tentatively.

"Here." He handed her the letter while manoeuvring a seat for her.

The two sets of pained eyes watched as Dee scanned the words. They watched as her eyes filled with tears. They watched as she mouthed the words as she read. "I will always love you".

She paused for a moment to look toward her two friends staring back at her. "What does that mean?" she begged them both for some reasonable explanation.

"There's more." Marco motioned toward the final line on the bottom of the page.

P.S. Always remember…home is where the heart is.

Once again, Dee mouthed the words as she read them silently. She repeated the words once again quietly in her head.

She glanced upwards at the two men as if searching their faces for recognition. She read the words once more, only this time out loud, "P.S. Always remember, home is where the heart is."

A smile crept onto her weary face. Her eyes alight with the memory of where she had heard those words recently. The conversation she had shared with her best friend, Kasie came streaming back into her consciousness. She stood from her chair and looked at her friend once more. Looking directly into his deep green eyes she once again repeated the words.

"Home is where the heart is!"

She locked eyes with him. "It's you, you are her home, the line, home is where the heart is describes you. She is telling you that her home is here with you."

He stood up and walked toward Dee. "What do you mean, what are you saying?"

"Remember I told you before… girls talk? Luckily for you though, because she told me exactly what this saying meant to her just the other day. She said she worked it out for the very first time just a few nights ago."

Dee paused to remember the exact words Kasie had used to describe her realisation from days earlier. "She said that laying on your chest on the daybed the other night after you had told her you loved her. She said that she realised that home is where the heart is. She had been homesick for Australia for a long time but she had a moment of clarity when she realised that home wasn't a place. That home is a person… and at that exact moment she realised her home was here with you. That you were that person."

Dee turned her attention to the man her friend had fallen in love with. "You are her home now. She wouldn't leave you. She loves you!"

She turned her attention to Marco. "I don't think she has left, or at least not of her own accord anyway," Dee added. "I don't believe she left Coral Cove willingly and I think this note is her way of trying to tell you that."

"It doesn't make sense," her friend challenged her. "Why would she write a note telling me to not follow her if she didn't want to leave me?"

"She is telling you not to try to fly to Australia searching for her, because she isn't there. She can't tell you where she is, but she is telling you where she isn't," Dee explained further.

"We can sit and hypothesise all day, it isn't going to do any good unless we have more information," Dee explained. "Why don't I get some coffee and we can start putting the pieces together." As she stood, she walked toward her heartbroken friend and handed him the note. "Please re-read it, but this time imagine she doesn't want to go."

He took the note and once again walked through his house and onto the pool terrace. He found his position on the daybed and unfolded the now crumpled piece of paper. He read the note, taking in the words carefully one more time. He paused and then re-read the words again. He closed his eyes and imagined her there with him lying beside him.

Having nothing but a small throw covering them and a few solitary candles throwing a glimmer of light onto their faces, he pictured the two of them huddled there in each other's arms. He told her the words he had wanted to say for years and she responded with the most beautiful three words back. He professed his love to her and as she lay there asleep in his arms he allowed his mind to imagine the promise of the future ahead for them. His memory of that night gave him hope, even if it was just for a moment.

He re-read the words. *I need to go home. Please don't follow me.*

If home really was with him, it made sense that she was telling him not to follow her to Australia. It made sense that she was giving him some clue that she hadn't left him to return to her family in Far North Queensland.

He looked skyward in thought, his eyes temporarily blinded by the bright morning sun. He was beginning to let himself believe that Dee was right, that the woman that he loved didn't leave him willingly. Which meant only one thing. His chest tightened as he imagined the only other reasonable explanation. And that was that Doctor Chris Bartlett had once again managed to find her and he was holding her against her will.

The fury swept through his body at the thought of the woman he loved held hostage by that crazed psychopath. Carrying the note in his hand he headed to his room to get dressed. He needed to find her and find her quickly before anything could happen to Kasie.

Having changed quickly and returned to the ground floor of the enormous mansion, the three friends began to piece together the details of the previous day.

Dee was holding court with the two men in the main office by the grand entry of the mansion. "Now let's think," she began, "How could Doctor Chris have found her? Could he have been following us the whole day waiting for her to be alone for a moment? But why would she leave with him? Without screaming, without trying to run away? There was no sign of a struggle in the house. There is no way she would have voluntarily gone with him." She paused.

"What are you thinking?" Marco asked her, sensing that a new theory was brewing.

"Her last words to me, were asking me to give her some time to find the words to come back here and tell…" She looked at her friend. "To tell you she might be pregnant… to Doctor Chris."

"I can't imagine how much anguish she was feeling," Marco empathised.

"What did she think I would say or do?" his boss asked Dee gently.

"I don't think she was worried about that, it felt to me more as if she didn't want to disappoint you. I am so sorry."

Dee slumped her head in despair. "I tried to get her back into the car, but she said she just needed a few minutes. And it literally was just such a short time between leaving her sitting on the edge of her bed and going back into the house to retrieve her."

"Chris must have been in the house," Marco added.

"Oh, that gives me the creeps just thinking about it." Dee shuddered as she spoke. It made sense to her though. It was the only plausible way for him to reach Kasie and lead her from the house in the short time that he had to act. Dee continued to formulate more of a theory, adding more and more details to what might have been Kasie's final moments in the house with Doctor Chris.

"If he was in the house, then he might have heard us talking. He might have heard her talking about the chance of being pregnant and coming back to tell you," Dee expanded on her developing theory of events.

"Which means he might have used the baby as a threat against her," Marco added.

"Which would also mean she would rather go willingly than let him drug her and potentially harm the baby," Dee suggested.

"I can't believe this. I can't believe she has had to go through this all alone again." Their friend finally spoke, adding to the gruesome picture they were forming.

He paused for only a moment, the devastation of the chain of events they were putting together sprung him into action. "Marco," he ordered, "you will need to question Anthony again. He must have heard or seen something."

Marco nodded in silence.

He continued. The clarity was returning to his sharp business mind as he began to plan his investigation. "Did everyone at the research facility, everyone that worked with Chris and Kasie get interviewed yesterday?"

"Yes. All of them." Marco didn't delay in responding.

"What about the two young interns?" Dee enquired knowing that these were the two girls that initially raised the alarm to Kasie about Doctor Chris's evil scheming.

"Yes, but my understanding was that they were both too emotional to provide much useful information," Marco replied.

"Then have someone interview them again. We are looking for every small detail they can think of, anything at all," his boss instructed him.

There was a sudden knock on the office door. The three friends were momentarily interrupted by the second in charge of security, James. "I am sorry to disturb you, boss, but Doctor Phoenix is here to see you."

"Thank you," his boss replied as he followed him out of the door.

"I have sent him to the upstairs office," James informed him.

"Thank you." The mansion owner made his way upstairs to the second floor of the enormous space he called home. The psychologist was ready and waiting for him.

"Morning," Doctor Phoenix offered his hand as his client entered the room.

"Morning Doctor."

"How are you holding up?" the Doctor asked, immediately entering into his assessment phase.

"I don't know, I just don't know." He lowered his head in despair. "If you had of asked me last night, I would have told you that I had ruined everything. That I lost the woman I love because I was overbearing, jealous and controlling. Today?" he paused, "Today, I don't know. Dee thinks that Kasie hasn't left on her own accord."

"Dee might be a good judge of what her friend would do. She was also the last person to see her from what I understand. Why do I sense you doubt that she might be correct?" the psychologist continued.

"I don't want to doubt. I want to believe she didn't leave, but the other side of that is if she didn't leave willingly, that she was forced to leave and the thought of that is just too painful to imagine right now."

"So, either option isn't one that you want to imagine?"

"I guess not."

"What would be your desired outcome to this scenario?" The psychologist challenged his client to articulate his innermost thoughts.

"That I find her today, safe and sound, unharmed and still wanting to be with me. That she tells me she loves me and I get to bring her back here to live with me safely. We plan a life together, a family. We both get our happily ever after."

"Sounds idyllic."

"It would be," his client agreed with him.

"What do you think would be her desired outcome?" the psychologist continued to probe.

His client was speechless. He hadn't yet managed to find out from Kasie how she felt. He assumed her feelings mirrored his own but he hadn't heard her yet say the words for herself. He knew she loved him; she had told him that much. But she had been reluctant so far to discuss the idea of marriage, or staying in Coral Cove with him and one day soon starting a family together. The two men sat together in silence both waiting patiently for the answer to arrive.

After some time, he finally spoke. "I guess I don't know. I know what I hope she wants but I don't think she has actually told me, not in her own words yet."

"Well that my young man, that is what you might need to find out, don't you think?"

"I guess so," his client reluctantly agreed, still absorbing the enormity of the psychologist's insightful but challenging instruction.

"There is one more thing to consider," The doctor continued. "Kasie has been through a horrific experience. One which none of us could say we could truly comprehend. She has potentially re-experienced this again if what Dee believes is true. My concern is that Kasie may begin to experience a form of trauma associated with these repeated abductions and druggings."

"Yes. I see. I completely understand Doctor."

"So, what I am going to suggest to you is that you give Kasie some time to move past this trauma. That time could be short. It could be days or weeks. It could be longer. It could take months, even years. Do you understand what I am telling you?"

"Yes, I think so," his client agreed, knowing he would do anything to help Kasie get through this nightmare.

"Ok, so either way the timeframe is totally dependent on the individual person's resilience, their coping mechanism and their supports."

"So, how do I best support her?" his client asked with genuine interest.

"Let her take the time, whatever time she needs. Don't rush her. Don't talk marriage with her. Let her come to that decision herself. And finally, don't rush intimacy with her."

"Oh," he said, feeling now very guilty for his heavy-handed tactics over the last few days. He had let his long suppressed sexual urges for her come to the surface and had been more than a little relentless in getting closer to Kasie.

Doctor Phoenix sensing his client's understanding continued, "Forget what has happened, just allow her to take the lead for a while. Talk to her lots, take the time to get to know one another again."

He didn't hesitate. He really would do whatever it took. "Yes, that makes sense. I understand what you are saying."

"Do you have any questions?"

"No, not at the moment, but I am sure I will. Do you think it would be best if you are there when we find her? Maybe offer to be there if she wanted someone to talk to?"

"I would be honoured to help. Just let me know where and when, I will make arrangements to be there."

The two men stood and offered their hands again in a formal but sincere sign of respect. The younger of the two men paused, holding his Doctor's hand in his just for a moment. "All I want is for her to be happy."

"I know, my son," The psychologist replied with sincerity. "I have known you a long time, I have known your wonderful parents too and trust me when I say that all I want, is for you to be happy too."

"Thank you."

"Anytime."

"I must go," the younger man continued, "I think we need to begin searching for her. I for some strange reason have this newfound energy to find the love of my life."

"Glad I could help then." Doctor Phoenix smiled a warm and knowing smile at him.

It was a busy day at the mansion as just as the owner saw his psychologist to the door and said his final farewells, another guest arrived. As fate would have it, just as Tiffany entered the mansion's grand entry Dee emerged from the office.

Dee was furious to witness Tiffany waltz through the door as if it was the most natural thing in the world for her to do. "Let me handle this," she demanded of her host as she marched toward the newly arrived guest.

"No!" her host stopped her in her tracks. "I will see her."

Dee looked at her friend with shock. "What is this about?" she demanded to know.

"Let me worry about that, Dee. I will only be a second, can you continue your planning. I will be right back." Her friend pleaded with her to let him handle this intrusion on his own.

Dee was uncertain and more than a little concerned about the reason for Tiffany's unscheduled and unannounced arrival but reluctantly allowed her host his privacy with her and headed back into the office.

The mansion owner looked toward Tiffany now standing hesitantly inside the grand entrance, just a few steps away from the massive wooden and glass front door that welcomed guests to his once alive and vibrant residency.

Tiffany watched the bachelor walk toward her, unable to make direct eye contact with him for fear of disapproval in his glare. She knew what she had done days earlier scheming her way into the mansion was wrong, but her desire to see him again overtook all reasoning as she plotted to gain entry into the four walls that housed the town's most eligible single man.

Little could she have known that he wasn't alone and wasn't available for guests. She felt ashamed for betraying his trust and wasn't sure how he might greet her. She watched him walk slowly, inching toward her finally stopping just a few centimetres away from her outstretched hands. She knew this wasn't a good sign. He would always greet her with a hug and a kiss on the cheek, but not this welcome.

He looked a mess, as if he hadn't slept or eaten for days. She wasn't quite sure what was going on except that she had heard that Kasie had gone missing. Some of the rumours had suggested she had gone home to Australia, others still hinted at something more sinister. Tiffany was at the mansion in the hope to find out more and to finally gauge the bachelor's plans for marriage and dating. Something she thought she would have found out at his birthday party the previous week.

Tiffany secretly felt extremely confident that she would one day live inside this very mansion with him. She knew she was the woman favoured by most to secure the promise of marriage from the wealthy town owner. She rationalised that given her current status she was well within her rights to arrive at the mansion today to offer her assistance in any way she could.

"I'm so sorry," she began. "I just heard the news and I wanted to come and see how you are and just say that I am so sorry for you."

"Thank you Tiff, that means a lot."

"Do you have any idea where she is or what might have happened for her to leave?"

He shook his head, not able to say a word in reply.

"I am so sorry. Is there anything I can do to help?" Tiffany searched his face as she reached out and took his hands in hers.

"I don't mean to sound ungracious but I have to get back to things," he apologised to her.

"Yes, of course, I understand," Tiffany responded. "Please just ring me if there is anything I can do to help… anything. I can't imagine how you are feeling right now. Plus, she is a friend of mine as well you know and I am worried about her too"

"Thank you," he added meaningfully as he released her grip on him and started back toward the office.

"Just one thing," Tiffany raised her voice slightly to ensure he heard her.

He stopped and looked back at the confident woman in front of him.

"We wondered why Marco was searching the wharf for Kasie yesterday. Did you have some reason to believe she might have been there?"

He was suddenly very interested in her next few words. This was a piece of the puzzle that he hadn't unearthed yet. He needed to know more. "Why do you think Marco was searching for Kasie at the wharf?"

Tiffany looked confused. "Well, because we saw his car there. You can't miss that sparkly brand-new BMW of his. I seem to notice it everywhere he goes. A few of us girls were having lunch on the deck at the wharf and saw his car going into the car park."

He watched Tiffany silently as she continued her story.

"It wasn't until later of course that we heard what had happened and it made me wonder why you would think Kasie was at the wharf. I mean I am assuming that was what Marco was doing there. Looking for Kasie. Am I wrong?"

Looking at her friend's perplexed stare, she wasn't entirely sure now that she had made the correct assumptions about the previous day's activities at the wharf.

"That is a very good question Tiff," was his cryptic reply to his unexpected guest. He walked toward her once more. "Thank you again. You have really been enormously helpful." He kissed her quickly on the cheek and headed with haste toward the office to share this new piece of information with his friends.

Tiffany watched him walk away and guessed that she wasn't going to get any further information from him today. She had hoped to be able to report back to Alice and the other women the latest piece of gossip coming from the mansion. But she was turned away empty-handed unable to go back and shed any light on the most recent drama unfolding in their town. She stood long enough to watch him return into the busy office.

He bounded through the large office door and without waiting for their attention, yelled toward his friend, "Marco, you need to get Anthony here now."

Marco and his boss seemed to now have a solid lead and were intent on questioning Anthony until they found out why he had taken Marco's car to the wharf when he was meant to be searching the streets of Kasie's local neighbourhood for her.

Dee could see the men were preoccupied with following up on this latest lead and felt that her time might be best served by heading to the research facility to catch up with Kasie's interns, Aretha and Annie. Feeling more than a little shaken by the recent events, she didn't want to venture out alone and found James who issued her with a security detail, a driver and a car.

"Don't be long," Marco instructed her. "And don't leave his side!" He motioned toward the steely looking man who was to escort Dee to the conservation society.

TWO

THE CLUES

The drive to the research facility brought the memories of the last twenty-four hours flooding back to Dee. She had last taken this route with her best friend Kasie beside her only the day prior. Enjoying their drive to Kasie's workplace and looking forward to catching up with colleagues, Kasie had been enthusiastic.

Dee remembered the drive back as very different. Dee initially joking with Kasie that she might be pregnant, a very flippant explanation for her ongoing stomach upset and nausea. Kasie at first shrugged off her friend's suggestion until a ghastly possibility entered her imagination.

Kasie began to fear that she might have been sexually assaulted by Doctor Chris, her abductor when he drugged her and held her hostage for the few hours she was asleep in the empty room at the research facility.

Having no memory of such a thing occurring it was only in the deep recesses of the mind that Kasie allowed herself a moment to consider this awful possibility. Putting their mind at ease somewhat by an impromptu visit to the hospital, the friends were left waiting for the results of a blood test. And then, Kasie's sudden and unexplained disappearance left them unable to hear the answer from the doctor that they were desperately waiting for.

The friends instead finding out the only good news of the day, later that night, that Kasie's pregnancy test had come back negative. She wasn't pregnant.

Dee had been so deep in thought that she hadn't realised that the car had pulled into the facility's car park until it came to a complete stop. She suddenly felt exhausted; maybe it was her body fearing that this was another dead end. She tried not to think so negatively. She had to hold on to the hope that Kasie was alive and unharmed and that along with the help of the two most determined and courageous men she knew they would find her soon.

She pushed herself to finally get out of the vehicle and began her search for clues. She had barely taken a step inside the door when she was inundated with questions.

"Have you found her?"

"Is Kasie ok?"

"Is she back home?"

Dee didn't know where to turn to begin to answer. She looked into the faces of the two young interns.

"Annie, isn't it?" She turned to the older of the two.

Annie simply nodded.

"And Aretha?"

"Yes?" Aretha responded.

Dee bowed her head, unable to look into the two innocent and very scared looking faces of Kasie's young staff. "I'm sorry, we don't know anything yet," Dee admitted in defeat.

A collective sigh was heard amongst not just the two young women but the other society staff now gathering around her.

Dee addressed the growing cohort. "I'm here to ask for your help. We have to imagine that someone knows something that can help us find Kasie."

Several pairs of eager eyes watched her as she spoke. "Is there somewhere we can go to chat?" she asked the growing crowd of concerned staff.

Aretha lead her to what Dee assumed was their conference room. A huge area overwhelmed by an enormous flat screen attached to the wall. A large round wooden board table stood in the centre of the room surrounded by very elegant slim white chairs. The room looked sterile, like something out of an action spy movie. The kind of room the secret agent would be summoned to in order to hear the evil villain's plan of world domination.

Taking in her surroundings, Dee was momentarily relieved of the heavy burden she was about to share with the group. Each person, one by one, took a seat around the table. Aretha, now standing next to Dee held out her hand as if to suggest Dee take a seat as well.

Dee sat, Aretha and Annie by her right side. The small crowd was silent, waiting for her to begin.

Dee looked briefly around at the anticipation on the faces in front of her. "Thank you for your time. It seems ideal if we could do this as a group. Let's put our heads together and come up with your best theories on where we could find Doctor Chris Bartlett."

The colleagues looked to each other and then again back to Dee. One by one they began to share their theories. They looked relieved as if unburdened; to finally be sharing what until this moment must have felt like idle gossip to them.

They each had their theories and each shared their ideas with Dee. The room was energised as every person wanted to do their best to help find Kasie, their much loved and respected colleague.

Making notes with a pen and paper Dee found in the middle of the board table, she wrote down every plausible detail and idea she heard. She even made note of those she thought were quite outside the realm of possibility.

The general consensus was that Doctor Chris Bartlett, the head of the conservation society had been acting even more unusual than was normal for his character. That was one point agreed upon by all.

Not many had any idea of why this might be so. Some workers spoke of late nights in the lab, their ideas relating to burnout or being over stressed and tired as a result.

Some even suggested improper use of legal and illegal drugs. Gaining this theory mostly from the deathly white glow the scientist so often possessed and his possible loss of weight and appetite of recent times.

All in all, Dee was forming a very interesting picture of the man who she had begun to believe without a doubt was holding her friend hostage.

"There's something else," Aretha added. "Eric Cobalt, we have seen that Chris met with Eric Cobalt recently."

"Who is he?" Dee's interest in this new player in the mystery was peaked.

"The tourism guy, you know the guy who owns the company who was granted the tourism contract."

Dee was curious. "And why would Chris be meeting with him?"

Annie was the next to add to the conversation. "That's just it, we don't know. He has no reason to meet with Mr. Cobalt, but they have met and spoken several times in the last few weeks that we know of. Maybe more even."

Dee paused to understand what she was hearing. "And did Kasie know about these conversations?"

"Yes," Annie continued. "We told her right before the first time she..." Annie paused before she was able to continue with her explanation. "Before she disappeared."

"Where is Eric Cobalt now?" Dee asked the group. "How could I find him?"

"He isn't a local. I think he lives in Europe or America somewhere," Aretha added. "He just has the business here but we normally never see him personally. He leaves his staff to look after the boats here for him. That is why we were surprised that Chris was meeting with him."

Dee continued to write down every last detail, not really knowing what was going to be helpful to the men leading the investigation or what they might have already found out from Anthony. Finally, Dee stood up from the large round table, keen to report back to the office at the mansion.

"I want to thank each and every one of you for your help. I promise to let you know the minute we find Kasie."

"We will be relieved to know she is ok," the distinguished looking older gentleman seemed to speak for the group."

"I promise I will let you know myself as soon as I hear anything."

The elderly man spoke again, this time with a slight sense of hesitation as if burdened by the question about to leave his lips. "Do you really believe that Doctor Chris has taken Kasie?"

Dee didn't know how to answer, she didn't know if she wanted to admit the answer to that question to herself or anyone else. It was the burning million-dollar question on everyone's mind. "I wish I could say no, but at the moment, it is our best guess that Kasie is with Chris." She paused for just a moment. "And I don't believe she would have left Coral Cove with him voluntarily."

Dee didn't waste a minute once she had jumped back into the car and the door closed behind her. She reached inside her bag for her mobile, looking at her handwritten notes in front of her as she made the call. She listened for the deep male voice to answer his phone.

* * *

Inside the Mansion, the two men were persistent in their line of questioning. Unable to get a clear rationale from Anthony as to why he was at the wharf the previous day, they continued their interrogation relentlessly.

The questions from the mansion owner were paused only for a moment by the ringing of his mobile. Always hopeful that the voice on the end of the line would be Kasie's, he kept his phone on him at all times.

He glanced down to see Dee's name. Looking toward Marco, he didn't need to explain to his friend why he was stepping outside the office to take the call.

"Dee?" Her name sounded like a half question, half plea as he said it.

"I don't know if this is anything, but does the name Eric Cobalt mean anything to you?" Dee gave the information without hesitation.

"Eric Cobalt has the contracts for the tourism boats for the reef. He isn't what I would call a scrupulous man but I highly doubt he would know anything about Kasie's disappearance," the male voice responded down the phone.

"Ok, so what if one unscrupulous man and another very unwell and highly dangerous man were to form some kind of sick alliance, what would you think then?"

He paused, putting the further puzzle pieces together. "Leave it with me," he said with absolute resolve. His tone lightened, "Are you on your way back?"

"Yes, I'm in the car, will be back soon." Dee met his concern with a direct answer knowing that he would be worried about her travelling around without Marco.

"Good, I don't like you being alone out there. I feel safer when you are here with Marco and I."

She thought about that for just a second. "Me too, trust me when I say, so do I!"

With a renewed energy and purpose, he returned his phone to the rear pocket of his jeans and walked back to the office where Marco and Anthony were waiting for him. He entered the room with such presence that both occupants stopped and looked. Knowing he had demanded their immediate and unwavering attention; he put on his best poker face and played the only hand he had in front of him.

"Do you know who that was on the phone, Anthony?"

Anthony sat silently, waiting for the answer to come from somewhere else. Finally, he shook his head to answer negatively.

"That was Eric Cobalt and he is demanding that you tell him where Kasie is right now."

The two men could see the panic as it rose in Anthony's face, his large round face turned a ghostly shade of grey. "But I thought she was with him," he stammered.

Marco couldn't contain his rage. He grabbed Anthony by his collar with one hand, clenched his fist in the other and hit the young man in the face. In a perfectly coordinated dance, the young man lost his balance, his chair falling back just as Marco let go of the collar and Anthony fell to the floor, blood gushing from his now swollen, red nose.

Marco reached down for his collar again, this time pulling Anthony from the ground with enough force that Anthony's feet were hanging inches above the carpeted floor of the office. Marco took aim once more, his clenched fist ready to strike again. Before he could make contact, the strong and monotone voice of his boss filled the room.

"Marco, put him down!"

Marco instantly obeyed his boss's commanding tone.

"I think Anthony is ready to tell us everything now." The tall dark-haired man looked at his young staff member, as he willed him to speak.

It had been enough to finally break Anthony. "I didn't mean for any of this to happen. He said he just wanted to talk to her. To give her information on the whereabouts of Doctor Chris Bartlett."

It took both men every ounce of strength to listen to the story unfold before them. Once promised a taste of their physical encouragement, Anthony told them everything. The call from Eric Cobalt himself, telling Anthony that he knew the whereabouts of Doctor Chris. Telling Anthony that he didn't trust Marco or the rest of the security team and that he would only share the information with Kasie herself in person.

Thinking this was their best chance of finally locating the man they had been searching for around the clock, Anthony organised for Eric to meet Kasie at her house. Keeping him in the loop of what time they would arrive, Eric promised he only needed a few minutes alone with her.

Anthony admitted he felt uneasy when the plan changed and he found himself collecting her note for his boss from the underground car park at the wharf. The way Anthony explained away his concern was to theorise that Kasie herself was following up on a lead and had written a letter to her boyfriend to let him know where she was going and why.

Anthony explained that he didn't begin to question any of it until that night and the discovery of the note by Marco and the reactions of the three friends frozen in the grand entry, each one appearing absolutely terrified at the contents of the handwritten letter.

Marco and his boss had few questions left to ask about the how or the why. All they wanted to know was where Kasie currently was, but Anthony had no further information to share with them. The two men wondered if Anthony yet fully understood the consequences of his actions. He was a young, ambitious man just starting his career with them but he appeared to have little insight into the damage he had caused.

Without any further clues from Anthony the two men were on their own again trying to source information on the whereabouts of any property or marine vessels registered in Eric Cobalt's personal or business names. Searching frantically for any information, the two men worked tirelessly stopping only as they heard Dee's voice as she walked through the grand entry.

Marco watched his boss stride through the office door bounding into the grand entry towards Dee. He didn't stop when he reached her, instead he held out his arms as he reached down for her, grabbed her into his arms and swung her around as if she was a weightless child.

Marco smiled to himself as he watched his boss plant kiss after kiss on her face, first on her forehead, then on her left check, then lips, then on the top of the head and right cheek. Dee swirled around giggling with glee at the obvious change in mood of the house.

When they finally stopped spinning and she had a moment to catch her breath she spoke, "We have good news then?"

"You are a genius!" he answered in reply. "A pure genius, how did you know?"

"Lucky guess, I think. Instinct maybe. So, where is she?"

Marco was the next to speak, "We don't know yet but we are getting closer… all thanks to you." His tone lowered as he moved closer toward her. Unlike his boss's moments before, his actions were slow and deliberate. He scanned her face for any reactions to the news as he reached out, grabbed her into his arms and hugged her tightly.

Dee allowed herself to relax into the hold, feeling safe and hopeful for the first time that day. She was holding up ok. She drifted further and further into Marco's warm embrace as if it was the lifeline holding her upright. Content to stay there a moment or two longer she was slightly irritated by the abrupt, loud and commanding disruption to her few moments of peaceful bliss.

Their boss had returned to the screen and obviously found the information they had been searching for. He had begun barking orders to his head of security staff.

"James, get the boat and helicopter ready. Marco alert the others we are heading for the wharf. Dee, you stay here." He paused and then thought to add further clarification to the instruction. "Dee, stay in the house until we return please."

"Yes boss," she replied sarcastically. "As long as you return with her," Dee's tone softened with the request. She knew these men would not stop until Kasie was found. She knew also that although shaken up and possibly drugged again, Kasie would be alive. It was the one thing she held onto. That Doctor Chris was madly infatuated with Kasie and the last thing he would to do once he finally had her to himself was to kill her. She knew Kasie would ensure she stayed alive, doing whatever she needed to. Knowing that her men would not rest until they found her and brought her home safely.

Her host looked her straight in the eyes again. "I will, I promise you I will bring her back."

Marco finally released his grip, gave Dee a peck on the cheek and went about his business. James having already left the grand entrance could be heard yelling instructions down his mobile.

It looked to Dee like it was all systems go. She decided to head to the kitchen to see if she could locate a hot coffee. She figured it was going to be a long day and night.

THREE

THE YACHT

Kasie wasn't sure how long exactly she had been on the yacht, *The Kingdom*, once more alone with the very dangerous Doctor Chris Bartlett. She didn't think it had been that long, but then again she had a habit lately of falling asleep at the drop of a hat. She knew the previous drugging had caused ongoing complications; that was to be expected. She knew that it would be easy for her to fall asleep and stay in a deep sleep for hours at a time. It was her body's way of healing and a sign that she was recovering. She wasn't sure if she had simply drifted off for a quick nap or had indulged in an intense twelve hour long deep slumber.

She was aware that at the very least she was still in the bedroom Chris had assigned to her and in the clothes she had worn onto the boat. Both conditions she thought to herself were positive indicators that he had not harmed her. She didn't remember being drugged this time and she didn't feel any aches or pains that weren't there previously, so another two welcome and very positive signs for her.

She sat up and did a mental scan of her body. She felt well, still a little nauseous but definitely better after her sleep. She felt frantically for the area around her shoulder blade, the area once the site for the deadly tracking device Doctor Chris had planted on her. There was nothing there except the red, healing scar of her previous injury. She was happy to be unharmed and eager to begin to formulate her plan for escape.

Kasie's eyes searched the cabin, no sign of him. No sounds either, come to think of it. This was getting better and better. Her stomach growled and cramped. She instinctively placed her two hands on her flat, toned abdomen.

She remembered Chris's last words to her. She recalled the look of disgust on his face when he assured her that he wouldn't be interested in touching her in any way as long as she was carrying another man's baby. He was a man of his word at least.

She smiled at the memory of it. The realisation that Doctor Chris thought she was pregnant and he had no hesitation in assuming that the baby wasn't his. There seemed little doubt in his mind that someone else was the father.

Another bonus, Kasie thought to herself. *That means I can't be pregnant.* But letting him find that out would place her in a very dangerous situation indeed. She figured she would let him believe she was carrying another man's child for as long as humanly possible. It might be the only thing keeping her safe at the moment.

That realisation that she wasn't pregnant was enough for her smile to turn into a giggle and then a reassuring laugh. Her stomach growled again, this time she recognised the feeling. She was hungry.

She wondered if this indeed meant that she had been asleep for twelve or more hours. Highly likely given her recent health concerns she thought. And given that being on the ocean, swept along by the currents while the waves slapped the side of the boat- her ideal sleeping conditions, it was a real possibility.

Her mind continued to wonder. "But if I have been asleep for twelve hours, where is Chris?" She said the words out loud as if saying them silently wouldn't thoroughly encourage an answer to her query. She wondered where he was and why he wasn't guarding her. Well maybe he was, she thought, maybe the slimy, creepy little man was just outside her cabin door.

She got up to explore the possibility. "Oops, must find a bathroom," she said again to herself. She walked into the cabin ensuite and considered for a moment the possibility of escape through the bathroom hatch. She stepped onto the toilet seat to peer outside through the yacht's rectangular hatch. She could see nothing but clear blue sea right through to the horizon.

She stretched her neck further into the fresh sea air. Nothing, she couldn't see a single thing, and strangely enough the only thing she could hear was the low hum of the engine as the boat pounded against the choppy sea. Did she just imagine it or did things just start to get even more rough? The yacht, which should have been smoothly sailing along the water with the wind available was rocking quite furiously against the choppy waters under motor.

She was always one to find her sea legs quickly so either way it didn't bother her but she wondered why they were moving so slowly. She wondered if the dangers of the rough open waters were making Chris a more cautious sailor than he might normally have been.

She decided that she would make her way on deck to check out the weather conditions further. She figured the fresh sea air would wake her up a little bit more before she began her search of the boat for food. She cautiously opened the cabin door and to her surprise her captor was nowhere to be seen.

Her heart raced for a moment at the opportunity for an escape. She was silent, listening intently to locate his whereabouts. Still nothing, there was still no noise, no movement from inside the boat. She made her way through the galley considering for a second whether she should eat now while she had the chance.

But her curiosity got the better of her and she continued through the galley past the dining area, up the few stairs and into the first lounge area. Her mind was racing with questions, so many questions. *Where was Chris?* She still couldn't hear or see any sign of him.

With caution, she continued her ascent through the lounge area heading for the deck. She allowed herself to take in the sound as her bare feet landed softly on the warm wooden deck. She took a deep breath of the fresh sea air and closed her eyes.

She sighed out loud. She loved being on the ocean. This was where she felt at ease, felt at home. She thought for a moment. This would feel like home if only… she stopped herself at the reality of the next few words and the pain that would bring her to think it out loud. She stepped further onto the deck, fully embracing the morning sun and feeling for the first time the wind that tore past her.

The boat bumped again, a loud crash of a wave against the bow hinted at the reason. She pushed through the wind and headed further out onto the deck in search of Chris. She imagined she would find Chris at the wheel, not doing a very good job mind you of navigating them to who knows where he was taking her.

She felt a strange sense of ease as she made her way out and into the sunshine. It was hard initially to place this sense of ease but she felt it must have come from finding the setting strangely comforting. Not the thought of being there with Chris of course but of being on the ocean. Hearing the wind gust past her, feeling the rocking of the boat against the strong ocean waves, knowing that beneath her and all around her were the gorgeous marine life that she was so intent on saving. She truly loved being on the ocean.

Being on the boat and sailing on the ocean felt so natural to her. Kasie climbed the last few steps still holding on the rail. She stood for a second, frozen in shock.

She looked forward at the boat's wheel and then for some reason at the huge leather couch behind it. She then turned her attention to the few stairs she had just climbed. "Where the hell is Chris?" she asked the empty deck.

* * *

The whirring of the helicopter blades was of no distraction to him as he pressed his lips to Kasie's. He couldn't hide his joy at finding her alive and unharmed. He ran his fingers through her hair until his hand found her cheek. He held her face against his and allowed his lips to devour her mouth.

He felt her moving with him, her hands over his body searching, frantic to touch him. He held her face in his hands as he released her from his mouth. He searched her face for her beautiful blue eyes as he mouthed the words, "I love you Kase."

A sudden jolt of pain rose up his shin and into his knee. He was awakened to the familiar laugh of his companion.

"I hope you weren't dreaming of me there, buddy," Marco laughed as his foot reached over to kick his friend awake once more.

"No one would be dreaming of your ugly face," he replied in jest.

"Dreaming of Kasie again hey?"

His friend didn't reply but instead turned his head to once again search the sea below them.

"Hey don't worry boss," Marco assured him. "We are going to bring her back. And don't feel bad about sleeping. It's no wonder, you have hardly slept in weeks now."

He looked at Marco silently as if to say thank you. The unspoken words between them a by-product of years of close friendship. Years of familiarity that had grown between the two men, born from their shared sense of values and enormous respect for each other.

"Marco, we are nearly at the boat," the pilot informed his passengers. "But there is something odd going on," he continued.

"What?" His boss was straight to the point wanting the latest update.

"The yacht has changed direction. It is heading straight for us."

The sound of the helicopter blades was blocked out by the noise cancelling headphones but that didn't stop him from thinking he heard the pilot wrongly. "What is it doing?" he asked Marco.

Marco made a childish hand signal to match his words. He steered and directed his hand as if it was a toy boat in a bathtub. "The yacht has changed course. It is heading back in the direction of Coral Cove." He loved to try to find the humour in any situation. He felt it to be an unofficial duty of the role.

"But why?" was all his boss could ask. There seemed no logical explanation to the change in course. If Doctor Chris did have Kasie on board they couldn't explain any reason as to why he would suddenly decide to return to shore.

Silently Marco shrugged his shoulders as if to answer… no idea.

The panic rose inside the two friends in equal measure. Neither were sure if this was a positive or negative sudden change in events but both felt the urgent need to reach Kasie quickly.

* * *

Back on board the yacht, relieved to find that the boat was on autopilot, Kasie continued her search for Doctor Chris. She had noted her current bearings and then left the boat to continue on its way. Having a quick look ahead of her and around her in all directions, she could see that they were some way from land.

Having scanned the deck, the lounge areas, and even the galley once more, Kasie continued back through the boat to search the rear cabins. There was only one place left for Kasie to look. She walked toward the master bedroom; its door shut tight. From the unknown void behind the sturdy timber door there was not a sound. The room was silent.

Kasie knocked. She heard nothing. She waited for just a moment until her curiousity got the better of her. She paused then knocked again. She thought she heard a vague soft sound that resembled a mumbling. She pushed open the timber door quietly and carefully peered inside.

The cabin was spacious and luxurious. Shiny wooden wardrobes were to the left and right of the bedroom, large enough to house her entire clothing collection. A door leading to the master ensuite was hanging open and swinging from side to side with the sharp movements of the boat. Windows and curtains all open letting the natural sunlight radiate through the room.

In the centre of the cabin was the master bed. A king sized beautifully appointed masterpiece of elegance and sophistication. The light shone miraculously on the bed to reveal the room's sole occupant. A small balding, grey haired, pasty skinned middle-aged man curled up in a ball. Kasie immediately entered the room and walked toward him.

"Chris?" Again, there was no response. "Chris, are you ok?" she questioned the quiet, still man on the bed.

"Sick, so sick," he finally managed to mumble back at her.

As if by instinct Kasie knew what to do. "I'll get you something for it," she told him. "I'll be right back." Without hesitation, Kasie headed to the galley in search of seasick medication or at the very least something to ease his nausea.

Kasie quickly located the boat's first aid kit and began searching for the right medication. As she held in her hand the anti-nausea medication, considering the contents of the small bottle, it suddenly dawned on her. She glanced back to the now open cabin door.

Her mind was steady and clear, giving her body simple step-by-step instructions on what it required her to do. She placed the medication on the sink and made her way quietly back into the master cabin once more.

Kasie placed her head just inside the door and whispered his name. "Chris?" As she suspected there was no reply. This man, her once trusted colleague turned abductor had the worst case of seasickness she had seen in her entire career on the water.

She very slowly tiptoed into the sleeping man's cabin and headed for the black overnight bag left on the chair beside the entry. She knelt on the floor in front of the chair so as not to be detected and began a quiet but methodical search of its contents. It didn't take long for her to locate what she was searching for. She opened the zipper on the small black hard-cased bag inside.

She flipped the bag open to display a very neatly and expertly arranged array of needles and vials. It sent a shiver up her spine to realise that these were the drugs intended for use on her once again. She knew as much because Chris had threatened she either come with him quietly or he would be forced to drug her yet again.

She read the labels carefully, some not baring much meaning to her at all. She read each one until she found what she was looking for. "Aha!" she said quietly to herself on finding the precious cargo. Without delay, in case her sleeping colleague woke before she had completed her mission, she expertly inserted the syringe into the glass bottle.

Now standing, she began to walk toward the bed, the needle in her right hand, paused but ready for insertion. She walked toward the sleeping man. She placed her left palm gently on his shoulder. "Chris" she whispered in his ear.

Unable to lift his head to speak, he opened his eyes ever so slightly and grunted something indistinguishable in the English language.

"Chris?" she said more forcefully this time. "Where is Dee?"

Chris could barely lift his head. His face had turned a shade of grey with a slight green tinge. He didn't look a well man.

"Chris, I am going to help you, but I want to know where Dee is first."

Chris's eyelids flickered ever so slightly. His thin lips parted just enough to allow the few words to leave his mouth. "I don't know. We don't have her. We never did."

Kasie let out a small sigh. She was relieved beyond belief that her friend was as far as she could guess safe and well. As promised, she delivered the medication to the ailing Doctor.

"Chris, I have something for you."

He looked at her but said nothing more.

"Here you go. I have just the thing for you." She held his arm in place as she placed the needle into the flesh of his shoulder. Chris didn't move or utter another sound.

Kasie replaced the used needle into the bag and raced back to the wheel of the impressive yacht. She noted their current direction, turned the auto pilot off and with expert precision turned the boat around. Once she was satisfied with her plotted course, she hoisted the sails and turned the engine off. The streamlined yacht performed exactly as it was meant to. It tilted into the wind and set off. Kasie smiled a little, wondering how Chris might have enjoyed this new ride but doubting very much he would even be aware of where he was right now.

* * *

"There it is!" Marco yelled through the headset excitedly.

His boss looked down at the yacht sailing its lonely course. It looked deserted, abandoned even. There were no obvious signs of life aboard.

"Can you get closer?" he instructed the pilot. With precision the helicopter dropped for a closer examination of the vessel.

"It looks to be at sail, engines off, but I can't see anyone," Marco offered.

"Me either. Do you think this is it?" his boss asked.

"Only one way to find out," Marco smiled at his friend.

"Ok," his boss agreed. "Let's do this."

Marco looked toward the co-pilot who had turned around to view the two men. He nodded to him. The co-pilot nodded back. Without another word the chopper moved toward the front of the vessel and made its descent. The two men glanced at each other one last time before they proceeded to jump from the chopper and into the deep, rough water below.

He plunged into the warm water and surfaced within a second to make his way to the sailing vessel. He knew time was of the essence. He glanced toward the boat between strokes, getting closer with each movement. As he neared the boat he stopped momentarily to witness Marco staring back at him, having already swum to the boat he was now staring back at his friend, a wide beaming smile etched on his face.

He continued his last few strokes to join his friend on the ladder attached to the back deck of the luxury yacht. Expecting Marco to be already storming the boat, he felt a strong sense of frustration at the strangeness of the situation unfolding around him.

He looked toward Marco. "What is that stupid grin for?"

Marco didn't respond with words, instead motioned for his friend to glance upward to the person standing at the edge of the stern of the boat. He looked skywards and could hardly believe his eyes, or his ears at what he witnessed next.

Kasie was staring down at him, her face looked relaxed, her eyes alight, her long blonde hair blowing in the wind. He watched as a strand of stray hair swept past her face catching her moist, plump lip. She lifted one single finger to remove the offending strand. He watched intently as her mouth formed a smile, her white teeth glistening in the sun. He watched her mouth as it opened, about to form a word.

"That was amazingly sexy" was all she had to say to them.

The two men scrambled onto the boat, without removing their wetsuits or stopping to dry themselves they both moved towards her. They tried to make sense of the bizarre scene. Marco took a step back, allowing the lovers a moment to take in each other.

"Are you ok?" her boss asked her.

"Don't I look ok?" she answered back, flirting just a little.

"You look gorgeous, perfect even." So many questions filled his head. "Have you been hurt?"

"I'm fine," she smiled back at him. "Actually, better than fine. It's true what they say, revenge is sweet."

He didn't quite understand what the implication of her statement was but he knew that she was happy, healthy and looked unharmed.

Marco interrupted the couple to step forward and give Kasie a quick but firm hug. "Where is Chris?" he asked her.

"He's sleeping. He's in the master cabin, but I don't expect him to wake anytime soon."

Marco felt confused by the strange situation. "But how?"

Kasie smiled a wide smile. "It would seem that Chris isn't quite the sailor that he might have imagined himself to be. He must have got seasick the moment the boat hit open water."

Both men stood before Kasie listening with silent anticipation.

"I think I slept for the first twelve hours I was on the boat, when I woke, I found Chris sick, unable to even stand. So, I did the only thing I could to help him out." She paused and smiled again. "I gave him a little of his own medicine, literally, I gave him something to ease the pain and help him sleep a little."

Both men looked at her then at each other.

"Don't worry," she continued. "He will be fine, probably better than he would have been if he had continued to be sick. He will wake up rested but slightly dehydrated I would imagine."

"What about Dee, is she with you? Is she ok?" Kasie questioned the men.

"She's fine, she has been with us the whole time," Marco assured her.

"She's actually the one who found you, the little detective that she is," his boss added.

Kasie felt an overwhelming sense of relief. Marco having gained the necessary information took his leave to check on Chris in the master bedroom.

The lovers were left alone, standing on the sunny, windy deck of the luxury yacht.

Kasie was the first to break their unusual silence. "Well aren't you going to give me a kiss hello?" she flirted with her handsome friend.

He didn't need to be asked again, he stepped toward her, grabbed her waist with his still damp right arm and drew her close to him. He kissed her lips. She moved even closer raising both of her hands to his face. The kiss was sensual and loving but quick.

He held her and looked at her questionably. There was one more question that needed to be asked. "Did he hurt you?"

"No, not at all. He didn't come anywhere near me. He must have got sick straight away." She smirked at the thought of karma giving Chris back some of his own medicine.

He sighed and bowed his head with relief. He thought now was as good a time as any. "Kasie, I know about the pregnancy test and…"

She didn't let him finish, "False alarm," she smiled at him. "Chris somehow knew of the pregnancy scare and was certain it was your baby. There was never a possibility of me even being pregnant."

"Yes, Doctor Harris confirmed it was negative."

"Great." She tried to smile at him, but he remained aloof. His head was downturned and he looked uneasy.

"Is there more?" she asked him, feeling a little anxious at the possibility.

He was hesitant to speak further. He remained silent while he gathered his thoughts. "It's just, when I read your note, I…" He paused. "I initially thought you had left me."

Her heart melted at the pain she had caused him. "I am so sorry. I never wanted to hurt you. I didn't have a choice. He told me that he had Dee and that if I didn't want her to get hurt that I needed to do as he instructed. I couldn't see any other way out."

He didn't respond, instead stood before her looking like a broken man.

"Hey," she tried to grab his attention with the lighthearted encouragement. "I knew you would come. That is why I started sailing back. I knew that you would find me. I wasn't quite sure if the helicopter was yours, they all kind of look the same to me, but the minute I saw my two men jump out of the chopper and into the open sea to swim to a moving boat, I knew then that it was you."

His downturned face turned towards her.

"Who else would be mad enough to do that?" she jokingly challenged him.

A smile finally emerged on his face. "Marco's idea of course."

She leant towards him to whisper in his ear. "And it was the sexiest, hottest rescue I have ever seen."

His smile widened as his eyes now found hers. "You like the action hero stuff then?" he flirted back.

"Oh yes," she whispered. "It made me feel like a damsel in distress, being rescued by my very own secret agent. Very sexy indeed," she added again.

He seemed to be eating up her encouragement and the tension was easing from his face. "What are you going to do with me now? Whisk me off in your helicopter to some remote island?" She laughed at the thought of it.

"Not quite, but would a boat do?"

"That would be perfect," she said as she leaned forward and kissed his salty lips one more time. "More than perfect actually."

Their kiss was interrupted as the sound of the boat engine coming closer broke into their quiet sanctuary.

Marco having heard the engine as well emerged from inside the boat to rejoin his friends. "Are you sure he is alive, Kasie? He's not moving," he asked.

"I don't care if he is alive, Marco!" His boss hissed at him. His sudden rage brought on by knowing they now had the man who had tried to kill the woman he loved. "In fact," he stopped mid-sentence as he began stomping towards the doorway. It was obvious to both of his friends what he intended to do once he reached him.

"No you don't boss," Marco ordered him as he reached out and grabbed his boss's upper arm. He didn't want to have to explain a dead scientist when he returned back to Coral Cove. "You have your hands full already. You need to take your lovely fiancé back home."

"Fiancé?" Kasie laughed at them both. "Just when did that happen?"

Both men turned toward her, their serious faces both now smiling back at her.

"Go boss. I'm not going to tell you again." He had the look of a man who wasn't going to take no for an answer. "I got this."

All too quick to give up the fight for the realisation that he had somewhere else he needed to be, his boss turned to Kasie and said, "Well, it looks like I've got you. Want to get out of here?"

"Oh yes!" Kasie was quick to agree.

He turned once more back to Marco. "Are you sure you are ok?" he questioned him again.

"Yes, for the final time. I will see you back on shore," Marco sighed, seemingly tiring of the reassurance required on his behalf.

"Just remember though, if he happened to fall overboard and got lost at sea, there probably wasn't much you could have done to save him. His boss added halfheartedly.

"I'm search and rescue remember. Ha. I don't think that story would float. Pardon the pun," Marco lightheartedly joked back.

FOUR

THE RESCUE PARTY

Kasie was helped into the arriving boat by security detail, James and Anthony. She thanked them both and made her way to the small seat at the front of the tender. She was joined immediately by her lover who sat closely beside her. His arms wrapped tightly around her as if scared to let her go again.

"We are a little far away to get back to land in this in a hurry," she shared with him.

"Why are we in a hurry anyway?" he smiled back at her.

"No rush," she assured him. She was definitely in no rush to return to normality.

Kasie leaned in to whisper in hushed tones, "Should I ask why Anthony appears to have a broken nose?"

He leered as he looked back to Anthony then back again toward Kasie. "Best you don't ask."

Kasie knew enough already to know that her question wasn't going to be answered, not at least at that moment anyway.

He thought he should relieve Kasie of her curiosity and let her know what lay ahead. "We are heading back to our boat now. But I should warn you, there are a few people waiting on board to see you."

Kasie smiled at the words our boat, just as she secretly loved being called his fiancé. She hardly believed, that after everything, she was safe again in his arms. She stopped to take in the last few words of his sentence. It was the part of the statement that didn't sound as pleasant as the words, our boat. She wondered who was on board to see her and why.

"That sounds ominous." Kasie was a little hesitant to answer anyone's questions at the moment. She really just craved some alone time with her handsome rescuer.

"I hope it's ok. I brought Doctor Phoenix and Doctor Harris. I thought you might need or want to see them both. And of course, there's Dee. There was no holding her back. She is about as compliant at following directions as you are. I can see now why you two are friends. I had actually left her at the house, or so I thought until she bounded into the car to join us on our rescue mission."

"Oh, well that is ok then," Kasie replied hesitantly. She didn't like the thought of a huge fanfare on her return to safety. She had hoped she would just quietly slip back into Coral Cove unnoticed. Not much chance of that now, she thought to herself.

"And Helen as well, she was worried about you and thought that you would need some nourishment."

"Oh, and then there is James and Anthony, who have obviously joined the rescue party," Kasie added slightly sarcastically, nodding toward to the two men in the boat behind her.

"Yes, well, we also have a captain and a steward who I don't think you have met yet and also a couple more security as well, probably guys who you have already met at our house."

There it was again. Those magical words she had been hearing so often in the last few days; our house, our boat, our bedroom. This man wasn't afraid of commitment and seemed to already be forging a future for the two of them.

"Is there anyone left at the Mansion?" Kasie said in full irony.

"Believe it or not, that is full too," he responded. "There are a lot of people very concerned about you. I had to actually stop people from boarding the boat for fear it might sink. I'm sorry. If it is too much, I will send them all away."

"No, not at all, and please don't do that. I understand. I have caused a lot of concern for people and I understand that they just want to help," Kasie said with all honesty.

"You haven't done anything," her lover was quick to remind her. "Please remember that. It was that cretin, Doctor Chris who has caused this situation. You are the innocent victim in all of this," he tried to help her understand.

"Of course, it's all ok. I am ok. I am actually really good, believe it or not. I am looking forward to seeing everybody, and then after that…" She paused before continuing. "After that is all done, finally returning home." She looked into his eyes for reassurance that was what he still wanted too.

"Home? or home, home?" he asked hesitantly but needing to know what Kasie was planning to do.

"Home, home where my heart is. Home is wherever you are." She smiled into his beautiful face as she leant in for another quick kiss.

The huge cruiser suddenly appeared upon the horizon. She must have been preoccupied she thought, for them to be this close to it already. She marveled at the size and sheer brilliance of the magnificent vessel.

She looked skyward to see the helicopter, just moments earlier hovering above her sailing vessel, now securely in place on the helipad on the roof of the cruiser. She looked toward her handsome lover. "It looks so much bigger from sea level. I don't think you were in any danger of it overcrowding and sinking," she joked.

"Well, size isn't everything," he jested.

No sooner had the cruiser come into view before they had reached its stern. The two men performing security detail working with what she assumed to be the deckhand to secure the small boat alongside the massive vessel. The first person to approach the boarding party and rightly so was Dee.

Not one to wait for formalities, Dee jumped into the boat and into her friend's arms knocking her backwards with sheer force and onto the floor of the small tender. She rested on top of her best friend planting wet joyful kisses all over her face.

"You're back, you're back!" she screamed, as if the reality of her safe return was merely a wild fantasy rather than a structured and well thought through search and rescue operation.

"Of course I am back Dee, why would you doubt that?"

"Well just that you disappeared into thin air then wrote a note virtually saying that you didn't want anything to do with any of us and that you were returning home immediately without your best friend, that's why!" Dee explained.

"All of which you should by now know was none of my doing," Kasie replied.

"Yeah, well I will forgive you this once, but don't you dare let this happen again… understand?" She demanded an agreement of her friend.

"I promise, my life will now be utterly boring and dull, that is if I even decide to leave the safety of my house again," she joked.

A small cough from her male companion interrupted. "Don't you mean to say our house?" her lover corrected her.

"Kasie." The even stronger and more mature older voice sounded from the deck just above them. Doctor Phoenix looked toward her lover with the scowl of a disapproving father.

"Yes, of course," her lover corrected himself. "Your house, of course, whenever you feel ready to return that is."

Kasie found the interaction between the two men to be quite confusing. She understood the psychologist was a trusted and loyal confidant to her friend, having known his family and been a personal friend to his parents for many years. This dynamic though was new.

Normally her strong, values driven friend was extremely self-assured, probably coming from a lifetime of experience, education and unfortunately, great pain. He had the maturity of a man beyond his years, but here today she was witnessing the younger man being given a stern warning by his older adviser.

Dee interrupted the awkwardness with new line of questioning. "Where is Marco?" she asked.

"He's still on Eric's yacht," her friend replied.

"Where is Doctor Chris?" Dee continued with her questioning.

"On the boat as well, but don't worry, he is contained. Marco is fine. Marco is sailing the boat back to the harbour. The police will meet him there," her friend explained.

"Can I join him?" Dee asked without delay.

Kasie looked inquisitively at her friend. "And why would you want to do that?" she asked her. Kasie was still unclear as to the exact nature of Dee and Marco's blossoming friendship. She had missed the chance to question Dee further on what happened the night she stayed at Marco's, seeking solace from the business and drama of the mansion. Kasie wondered if maybe there was a slight chance of a relationship forming.

She smiled a little at the thought of it. A new connection with Marco might mean Dee staying in Coral Cove much longer than she had planned. Kasie felt quite sinister in hoping for this selfish desire but couldn't think of anything better than keeping her friend on the island for a while longer. She laughed as she fleetingly imagined the four of them residing in the mansion together.

Her daydream was interrupted by Dee's response to her valid question. "Well, so he is not alone," Dee answered in a very matter of fact manner.

Kasie and Dee together looked to their host for approval.

"Well, you would need to contact Marco first and see what he thinks of the idea. If he is ok with it, then it is fine with me."

"Thanks!" Dee responded, kissing her friend eagerly on the cheek.

"What about me?" Kasie asked her best friend, with a more than slight sense of abandonment in her voice.

"Kasie," Dee answered with just a single word, her head turned on the side as if to suggest some over dramatisation on her friend's behalf. "Don't you think you have enough people here that need to see you? Marco is on that boat, all alone with that psychopath," her friend continued.

Their male companion laughed. His head thrown back in the act. "You might think that Chris is the psychopath on that boat, but he is by far the less dangerous of the two men on board that vessel at the moment."

"I don't doubt that," Dee replied with a quiet confidence. "So, do you have an issue with me joining him?" She looked to her best friend for her approval now.

"No, be my guest," Kasie joyfully responded.

Kasie had barely made it out of the boat before Helen accosted her, the mansions head chef, coordinator and social events planner. The older woman was looking remarkably at home on board the massive cruiser. "Oh, Kasie," she began "are you ok my dear? You do look really well darling."

"I'm fine, I really am Helen. Thank you so much," Kasie politely responded.

"Can I get you something to eat? You must be starving." Helen was eager to ensure that Kasie was safe and well.

Kasie smiled at the kindly woman. "Actually, to tell you the truth I am quite hungry. If it wouldn't be too much bother, I would love something to eat and drink."

"Please, let me. I will be back in a moment." She began to head back to the galley before she turned once more to Kasie and asked, "Any requests?"

"Actually, if you have one, I would love a beer," Kasie smiled at her hostess.

"Could you make that two, please Helen?" their boss added as he now made his way across the back deck and toward the two women.

"I might even bring one for myself and join you," Helen laughed. "I want to hear all about this daring rescue."

"Please do," her boss answered.

"Be right back," she assured them both.

Just as Helen left, Doctor Susan Harris appeared. "Does he have you all on a rotating roster?" Kasie joked with the doctor.

"Not quite, but nothing would surprise me. How is our guest of honour?"

"Ha," Kasie laughed. "I am hardly that."

"Well?" the doctor continued, "Could you spare me a minute or two before you settle into your cold beverage?"

"Absolutely," Kasie agreed, following the doctor into what she assumed was her host's private quarters.

She looked around at the impressive surroundings.

The doctor took a seat on the cushioned leather lounge inside the huge bedroom. "Please take a seat Kasie, just for a moment," The doctor requested.

"Sure." Kasie sat down in place obligingly. "Is everything ok?"

The doctor smiled gently to reassure her patient. "So, I know you want to be out there and enjoying your freedom, but it is important for a number of reasons that we get some things sorted before you do that."

"What sort of things?" Kasie asked with some concern.

"Kasie, the last time I saw you, we did a pregnancy test and I need to let you know that the result was negative."

"Yes, I know. Doctor Chris admitted that he couldn't be the father of my child. He had heard of the pregnancy news and seemed to believe the only option for the father was his arch nemesis."

"Well that is good news, Kasie. I am so pleased to hear that for you," The doctor replied.

"So, can I ask a delicate question of you?"

"I think you are going to anyway," Kasie responded.

"I am sorry to have to ask, but did Chris physically harm you in any way?" the doctor asked quite directly but still with some hesitation.

"You know what doctor," Kasie responded "He was so sick that I didn't even see him. He directed me to my room, I must have fallen asleep and I awoke the next day to find him almost unconscious in his room. He was so sick he couldn't even stand, let alone drive the boat or hurt me in any way."

The doctor let out a huge sigh of relief. "That is wonderful news Kasie, but what about drugging? Did he inject you with anything this time?"

"Again, no, he told me which room was mine and that was the last I saw of him. I feel fine, I have no new needle marks, no headaches, no stomach cramps even, except I am feeling very hungry now. I feel really very good."

"Again Kasie, that is exceptional news. I couldn't have hoped for anything more for you. Is there anything at all that you want to talk to me about? Anything at all concerning you?"

"Um, no, not that I can think of at the moment. I guess. Um…" Kasie paused to consider her question. "I guess the only thing is, the drugs, the toxins and poisons that have entered my body in the last week or so… could that affect me falling pregnant in the future? Could they somehow affect my child if I was to fall pregnant?"

"A good question Kasie and I must admit that I don't have a decisive answer for you about that at that moment. I am still running tests at the hospital to try to determine what combination of drugs Chris used. But I will promise you that I will continue to research it until I can give you a more definite answer. Can I ask you, and please don't answer if you don't feel comfortable but can I assume from your question that children are something you see in your not too distant future?"

"Yes, I think so. Well I hope so. Not yet of course but some day," Kasie clarified for the kind doctor.

"So, can I be so bold as to ask, if our own Coral Cove heir might be future father material for any children you are thinking of having?"

Kasie let out a nervous giggle. "Doctor, could I assume that if I was to be pregnant tomorrow or even anytime in the future, that you would be my primary physician?"

"Well, of course I would be honoured," The doctor replied.

Kasie continued, "Would that mean patient and doctor confidentiality rules apply with us from now on?"

"Of course, if that is what you would want."

"I think so. And to answer your question regarding the heir of Coral Cove... Well really what woman in their right mind would not consider the possibility of children with that incredible man?"

"Well as your primary physician I would suggest the answer to that question to be none. As far I as I can see, there would hardly be a woman in Coral Cove who wouldn't accept a date with your lovely companion, let alone a marriage proposal with the promise of a family and future."

"Yes, well, I guess I have just become like every other woman in this town then," Kasie giggled as she found the humour in her own admission.

"Thank you Kasie, for trusting me," The doctor gently added. "I will make it a priority to get the final results and give you the reassurance that everything will be ok. Is there anything more I can do for you?"

"No Doctor, you have been amazing. I can't thank you enough."

"So, now that we have that sorted, do you think you would like to call me Susan?"

"I would love that, thank you Susan." Kasie stood and embraced the kind woman who had just become her trusted confidant.

"I will let you return to your welcoming party. Please call anytime. I will ring you as soon as I know anything."

"Thank you again Susan."

As Kasie emerged from inside the cruiser, she was surprised to find Helen taking in the sun on board the large back deck. She found ample seating beside the older woman on the white and turquoise coloured leather lounges.

"Are we missing someone?" Kasie enquired.

"I think he is with Doctor Phoenix," Helen suggested. "Should we wait?" she added politely.

"No, I think in all honesty, we both deserve this. I am sure he will be back soon."

Kasie grabbed her beer and raised it to Helen. The two women clicked the glass. "Cheers!" they sung out together.

"And here is to the first lady of the house returning home soon," Helen added.

Kasie nearly choked on her first mouthful of the tasty beverage. "Now, settle down Helen. Not so fast," Kasie laughed.

While the two women were enjoying their refreshing cold beers, their host was holding court with his psychologist inside the office on board the huge vessel.

"How are you?" the psychologist asked without delay.

"Confused I think," his client responded.

"Why is that?"

"I'm not sure, I'm not sure about anything anymore but I think I was preparing myself for the worse and then there she was, just as I had hoped, safe, well and unharmed."

"So maybe your princess, didn't need rescuing after all?" the psychologist challenged him.

"Well actually she was relying on it. Well not really, I guess, she seemed quite capable of making her way back to shore but she said she was expecting us, she didn't seem surprised at all to see us arrive in the chopper."

"Interesting, isn't it?" was all the psychologist offered in return?

"What does that mean?"

"What do you think that means?" the psychologist replied without answering.

"Seriously, I sometimes think that with the money I pay you I shouldn't be working so hard."

"Well, do you just want my advice?" Doctor Phoenix asked.

"Honestly, sometimes yes."

The psychologist thought about what would be the most relevant and pertinent response to his client's request. "Well, I think my original advice stands. Take it easy. Be aware that Kasie may be experiencing some trauma. Don't rush her. Let her take her time to feel safe with the world again. No talk of marriage or children, for now at least."

"I can do that," his client agreed without hesitation.

* * *

As he walked back down to the deck, he smiled as he saw the two women chatting away, drinking their beer as if nothing in the world was amiss. He couldn't believe how lucky he was to have her back. It felt like the perfect fit and now there was nothing stopping him planning a future with her. Except of course his psychologist's advice to let her take her time and not rush her.

Kasie turned to see her friend emerge from inside the boat. Helen followed her eyes to see their handsome companion walk toward them.

"Well about time," Helen joked, "I was promised a refreshing drink and here I am nearly finished by official break time and still only drinking my first beer."

He laughed at the refreshing simplicity of the situation. It was nice to just be able to be carefree once more. "Since when have you ever had official break times?"

"I am sure it was written into my contract somewhere," Helen responded.

"I am sure it was not," her boss joked back. "And besides, you should actually be on a month-long holiday in Tahiti right now. Maybe we should swing by there and drop you off."

"Oh Helen!" Kasie began, "Please tell me you didn't delay your holiday again?"

"No, no," Helen reassured her. "I hadn't booked it, your husband here is just dying to get rid of me, probably to replace me with a younger model while I am away," she laughed.

"Well, he isn't exactly my husband." Kasie paused as she looked sheepishly towards the god-like image standing above them. "But I can assure you that if I had any say, that you will always and forever be irreplaceable."

"I think I will enjoy working for you Kasie," Helen joked.

"Please, please," Kasie pleaded, half joking. "Give me a chance to catch my breath."

While the three of them enjoyed their second beverage, Kasie took in the peace and quiet of the sunset turning the open sky around them a gorgeous shade of pink.

"Am I just imagining this, or have the crowds disappeared?" she asked.

"Well actually, I think that they have in the most part. Dee got her approval from Marco and joined him on Chris's yacht. Doctor Harris and Doctor Phoenix took the helicopter back. I sent some security back to the house and some to check on Marco and Dee. Are you ok with that?"

"Of course, the quiet is really very pleasant," Kasie elaborated.

. "And on that note, I must start making some dinner." Helen excused herself as she stood and walked toward the galley.

FIVE

THE THEORY

The two lovers were alone, sharing in the beauty of the pink and crimson sky above the horizon. "Would you like to sit with me?" Kasie asked.

"Yes, of course," her companion answered hesitantly before moving to join her on the seat beside her.

Kasie sensed that something wasn't quite right with her friend. "Is there something on your mind?" she questioned him.

"No, nothing," he replied rather too quickly.

"Really?" she questioned. "Because in case you hadn't noticed I am a woman and women sense these kinds of things."

"I'm sorry, I guess I am just feeling a bit overwhelmed." He was silent for a moment as he searched for the best way to explain his current quietness. "This morning I thought you had left me and now you are here, watching the sunset with me."

"Well, I hope that is ok with you, because I imagine us sharing many more sunsets together."

This brought a smile to his face along with a small sigh.

"Are you sure you are ok?" Kasie questioned him further.

"Yes, of course," he responded as he wrapped his strong arms around her and she settled into her comfortable position beside him.

As Kasie glanced toward the sunset taking in the slight cool breeze on her face and the warm, hard and comforting feel of his chest against her, she recognised that familiar feeling of being at home. That sense that she was exactly where she needed to be in the world at this present point in time. A wonderful feeling, she imagined that she had maybe started to take for granted.

I wonder, she thought to herself, how many people actually felt this way before they decided to get married and spend the rest of their lives with somebody. For Kasie this was the first time in her thirty-four years that she had felt this way. Absolutely sure, one hundred per cent comfortable with another person, this wasn't something that happened every day. She felt incredibly grateful that she had found it.

"Maybe after we eat, we should turn in for an early night?" Kasie suggested.

"Yes, sounds good to me," he agreed easily. A room has been prepared for you and Dee brought along some clothes to make you feel more comfortable.

"Oh," Kasie replied. "So, are we not sharing a cabin tonight?"

"Well, I just imagined that you would want some time on your own tonight, you know without me harassing you."

"Really?" Kasie questioned him. "What would make you think that?"

"Is that not the case then?" he asked with some underlying confusion.

"Well, I thought I might get to fall asleep in your arms tonight," Kasie reflected.

He paused, seemingly unsure of what to say. "Well, I guess we are both tired, so maybe it is best for us to get some sleep and see how we feel in the morning."

Kasie was beyond hurt. She was confused and disappointed and saddened that something, somehow had changed. This wasn't the same man that had been kissing her in his office or pushing her against her bedroom wall full of sexual frustration that they could not be together. Was it possible that this was the same man that performed his whole tease, stripping down to his underwear and parading in front of her, climbing into the shower and encouraging her to step inside the bathroom and help him wash?

What had happened to him, she wondered, for him to become suddenly so distant? Was it the note, she wondered or was it that she had been alone with Doctor Chris and he didn't accepted her version of events; that nothing at all had happened between them? She started to feel a sense of rage and frustration rise in her body. She was angry with Chris for the potential damage he had done to her budding relationship.

They two enjoyed a hearty meal and a bottle of wine before retiring for the night. Kasie was still upset that her lover didn't appear to want to spend the night in his room together, instead encouraging her to use the master room as her own, taking one of the guest cabins for himself. By the time she was ready for bed, she had felt so tired again she couldn't muster the energy to argue anymore and instead crawled under the sheets and enjoyed the feel of the huge cruiser moving ever so slowly through the open waters.

Kasie emerged the next morning feeling refreshed, re-energised and ready to greet the day sailing on the gorgeous blue ocean that she loved. The first thing she noticed was that the cruiser was moving incredibly slowly, almost feeling like six or eight knots she thought. She walked toward the back of the boat to find her friend. As she emerged through the doors to the back deck, the most inviting image she had seen appeared in front of her.

There he was, her model-like companion dressed in knee length grey cargo shorts and a fitted white tee. No shoes, no watch, no phone, no staff or anyone else around him for that matter.

Just the man she loved standing looking out onto the ocean, a simple white cup of what she assumed was hot black coffee in his hand. The sun, lighting his body, shining brightly on his dark hair making it look like its sole purpose was to illuminate the shine and colour of his dark locks. His deeply tanned skin was absolutely glowing. He looked relaxed, comfortable and content. He hadn't noticed as she exited the back door and she paused for a moment taking in the gorgeous morning scene before her.

As if suddenly sensing he was being watched, her gorgeous man turned to look toward where she was standing. Catching her eyes, his face turned into one amazing smile, from the corners of his beautiful mouth to the glimmer in his deep green eyes.

"Good morning beautiful," he smiled at her as he made his way towards where she was standing.

"Good morning back, handsome." Her face too was beaming with happiness.

He placed his cup on the nearby table as he stretched out his arms and embraced his companion.

"Did you sleep well?" he asked her.

"I could say I slept like a baby," she was quick to reply. "But it could have been better if I wasn't all alone." She made a small pout with her mouth as if to elicit some sympathy from him.

"Mmm... Sounds like you are trying to tell me something."

"Maybe just that I would have preferred to have spent the night with you," she replied.

"Yes, well I guess I should explain that. I didn't sleep really well thinking about it and it might be best if we talk."

A slight panic raced through her head; her mind awash with possibilities of what he might want to talk to her about. Anxiety pulsed through her body, sending that familiar feeling of tightness in her stomach. She feared that she was about to hear that the man she loved had changed his mind. Maybe deciding that really all the drama wasn't actually worth it. That pursuing a relationship with her had been far more work than he had ever intended.

"Oh my god, please don't tell me you have changed your mind. Not after everything. I couldn't bear that right at this minute."

"Oh Kase, no!" he was quick to reassure her, "Never, I would never change my mind about us."

"Oh, thank god." She let out a huge sigh of relief. "Then what is it? Is it about Chris, because I swear nothing at all happened? I promise I would tell you if it did."

"No, of course not Kase. I trust you one hundred percent and beside even if it did, it wouldn't change us."

"Then what? What has got you acting so strange? So distant all of a sudden?"

"Kase, it is something Doctor Phoenix said to me. He has been helping me to know how to handle things, with all the drama with Chris and everything, and you being so unwell of late. I guess I have been trying to get some advice on how I can best support you."

"Really?" Kasie asked with surprise. "You have been asking Doctor Phoenix how best to support me? Why not just ask me?" she questioned him.

"Well I guess, I didn't want to burden you and I wanted to help you to recover and move past all of this as quickly as possible."

"All of this?" Kasie asked again, this time with a tone of frustration in her voice. "What exactly is, all of this then according to Doctor Phoenix? Please do tell." The sarcasm in her voice was impossible to misread.

Her companion continued, looking a little sheepish at the thought that he had been discussing her without her knowledge and also somewhat concerned at the outcome of the conversation. "Doctor Phoenix has been talking to me about how you may be experiencing some trauma. He said it would be normal and associated to the two abductions you have had to endure."

"Well did he now?" Her tone was unmistakable now. "And what else did our friend Doctor Phoenix say about me, without can I add, even talking to me about how I might be feeling?"

"Please don't be upset with him. He is only trying to help and I was the one who asked for his advice," he responded.

"Well I can't help but feel a little bit angry at the fact that you are getting advice about me, without information from me or even asking me what I want."

"I guess Doctor Phoenix was suggesting that given the trauma, you may not be the best judge of what you need right now."

"Oh, really now?" Kasie's anger was rising by the second. "Please share, please share this great man's words of advice to you."

He paused and swallowed hard. He realised the conversation was not going well at all. He wanted to end it there, to pretend he hadn't said anything but he knew Kasie and he had seen her like this before, normally when she was angry at Chris. He knew he had no choice but to continue to tell her everything.

"Doctor Phoenix said that the best way for me to help you was to take things easy." He looked at her for some indication at how she was digesting that small piece of information.

"And?" she simply said, "What does that involve?"

"Well, he said I shouldn't push the idea of marriage, children, our future for the time being and…" He paused, not really wanting to add the next piece of information.

"You know you have to finish that sentence?" she threatened him.

"And he said that I should not push you for intimacy at the moment."

"Are you serious?" she yelled at him. Kasie was furious. "Please don't tell me you have been telling the good old Doctor everything about our… our…" She didn't quite know what to call it. "Have you been telling him about us, have you?" She looked at him pleadingly, "Please tell me you haven't."

"It wasn't my intention," he replied with all honesty. "But with the pregnancy scare and me trying to explain that we couldn't be pregnant, some details just came out. I am so sorry Kase. Please forgive me." He looked at her with his best puppy dog eyes impression, hoping for her forgiveness.

Her heart instantly melted looking into his sparkling eyes, his downturned head, a small flicker of hair hanging dangerously close to his long dark eyelashes. His mouth as if impersonating her earlier pose, was doing its best pleading pout.

"Of course, I can't stay mad at you." She leant in to give him a quick peck on his outstretched lips. "But the Doctor Phoenix, he is a different story, where did that man get his degree from? The side of a Weetbix box?" She answered her own question.

"The side of a Weetbix box?" he asked looking puzzled.

"Sorry, that must be an Australian saying. I guess I was suggesting that his qualifications might be a little dodgy as a result of his flawed assessment skills."

"He said you might say something like that. That you might downplay everything you have been through."

"Did he just?" Kasie's fury was rising inside her again at the thought of the psychologist's harsh and inaccurate perception of her.

Her natural reaction to being told she was supposed to act a certain way, was to do the exact opposite. It was a form of defiance that she could recall having from a very early age. *I think I will just have to show the wise psychologist then,* she thought silently to herself. Thoughts of plotting began forming in her head as she turned to look at the now quite still ocean beside them.

She remembered her earlier question and again turned her attention to the gorgeous specimen of a man beside her. "I came out to ask, why are we moving so slowly?"

"We are nearly home already, the harbour is straight ahead." He motioned towards the bow of the boat and the shoreline coming into view ahead of them. "I thought you might want to take a leisurely cruise in and enjoy the best part of the morning on the ocean."

Pleased at the thoughtfulness of his actions Kasie smiled at him, "You know me so well already."

"Anything to make you happy," he smiled back as he leant down to kiss her on the forehead.

A thought jumped into her mind. She smiled a wicked smile as the plan quickly formed in her head. "I wonder, do you have to rush back?" she enquired.

"Not really, I mean no, not at all," he smiled back at her, seemingly excited to hear what she might be suggesting.

"Well it's just I had a thought," she continued, "I wondered if we might be able to spend a day or two on the reef." She looked into his eyes for her next words to make the maximum impact. "Just you and me, that is. Alone for a few days on the boat."

His smile beamed as he picked up the suggestive tone in her voice. "That sounds like a wonderful idea. I think I might just be able to make it happen." His smile left his face for a second as another thought occurred to him. "But that is as long as that is what you think is best, you know. Otherwise we could also ask Marco and Dee to join us so that you can feel safe."

"Oh my god, I swear!" Furious at the suggestion that she wouldn't feel safe alone with this man and outraged at the stupid psychologist for putting the idea in his head, Kasie turned to threats of physical violence. "I swear if you preach that stupid Doctor Phoenix's ridiculous theories to me one more time, you are going overboard. Do you understand?"

He laughed, finding her anger humorous and not at all having the desired effect of fear on him. "Yes, I get it." He was eager to follow through on her idea of a few days onboard the boat. "Ok, so

let's get these final few guests out of here and sail this baby to the reef.
I know the perfect spot."

SIX

THE SHARK

Having finally anchored up on one of the specially designed buoys that prevented further damage to the coral beneath them, they found themselves perfectly positioned just beyond the reef.

Kasie was pleased to find that despite the perfect weather, they were alone in the water today, not another vessel anywhere near them. It must be fate, she laughed to herself.

She took her towel and made her home for the afternoon on the large flat surface of the bow of the boat. She guessed it wouldn't be long before he joined her.

She lay down, dressed in a new white bikini that had somehow appeared in the bag that Dee had packed for her. She hadn't really thought about it before, but someone must have been shopping for her. Knowing that little by little new items had appeared in her bags and in her guest room, she wondered who the person with the exceptional taste was.

Her first guess was Dee, she knew her well, knew her style and her sizing, but she also realised that Dee must have been quickly running of our money. Not having been in Australia for some time now, she must be spending money she probably didn't budget on.

Kasie's wonderings were interrupted by her gorgeous companion who had come in search of her.

"May I join you?" he asked as he smiled down at her.

"I was kind of counting on it," she smiled back at him.

"I made you a cocktail," he said as he handed her a long, slim glass of an unfamiliar cold white beverage.

"Thank you," she politely responded as she accepted the glass from him. "Should I ask what it is?"

He smiled a knowing smile. "I believe it is called a milkshake."

"Is it a milkshake, not a cocktail?" She searched for clarification.

"No, it's a cocktail, lots of vodka in there. It's a recipe made with this new vodka everyone is raving about. I got the idea from Marco actually."

She took a long sip of the cold, refreshing drink. "Delicious," she drew out the word for extra meaning.

"I will have to thank Marco, this is incredible. A girl could enjoy these all afternoon. I better be careful not to drink too many or you might take advantage of me." She flirted with her words as she watched him enjoying a taste of his drink.

He looked toward her and with reassurance in his voice replied, "I promise I won't be taking advantage of you. You can feel safe knowing that I am happy to wait. We have all the time in the world. No rush."

Kasie was becoming increasingly frustrated with this new determination of his to take things slowly. Since waking from the cabin on The Kingdom and witnessing their daring rescue of her, she had thought of nothing else but being close to this incredibly sexy man once more.

She was angry beyond belief that a psychologist, a man who barely knew Kasie could give him advice on how to progress their relationship. For Kasie now, it felt like there was nothing else standing in their way. They had nothing holding them back and she needed things to progress in their relationship. She could readily admit, she wasn't ready to start planning a wedding, but she craved intimacy with the man she was quickly beginning to realise was the one she knew she wanted to spend the rest of her life with.

When he spoke to her, he appeared to be adding reassurance as if more to remind himself of his new improved behaviour than to comfort her. She imagined it was just as difficult for him to restrain himself as it was for her. Oh well, too bad, she promised herself. She was determined for that resolve to not hold for long at all. Looking toward him to ensure that he was in the perfect position to witness her next action, she began her plan of attack. She was now determined to finally seduce this man and make love to him for the very first time.

She placed her drink down carefully on the deck beside her, she took both hands and reached behind her back and found the string of her tiny white bikini top. With a gentle tug, she untied the string, letting the two halves of the string fall down her back. She then found the knot at the base of her neck. She again loosened the string and released her top from her body. She cupped the small material of the bikini in her hands, holding them in her palms for just a second she then removed them from her now naked breasts.

She didn't need to look. She could feel his eyes burning through her skin. She let out a seductive sigh and lowered her head onto the towel. Her back laid flat on the deck of the boat. She raised her tanned, toned legs at the knees and placed her feet squarely on the deck beneath them.

She knew this was the perfect position to show off her slim and tanned body. Her flat stomach lay glowing in the sun. Her slender legs were at the perfect angle to look feminine yet toned. She placed her arms against her sides, her palms flat against the deck. She closed her eyes and imagined in her head, the expression on his face.

"You're killing me here," she heard him whisper softly to her.

She didn't answer. She wanted to play innocent. She wanted to allow him to come to her. She lay still listening for his movements beside her. Willing him to touch her warm body. Feeling the urge inside her heighten as she waited to feel the electricity of his fingers on her skin. The wait was agonising. She listened intently for any clues as to what his next movement would be. She heard him let out a small sigh and move slightly next to her. Then he was still. Silence.

Not being able to stand the anticipation one second more, she glanced toward him. She turned her head ever so slightly and saw that he was laid down on his towel next to her. Almost mirroring her pose, he laid flat on his back. His strong, muscular legs stretched out flat beyond him. His head resting on his towel, his eyes closed. He appeared to be still, taking in the sun. Not looking as if he was about to move at all.

Kasie had to think of her next move. She knew her opponent would be stubborn but this was ridiculous. Kasie stole a sneaky glance at the body of the stunningly sexy man lying beside her. She noticed that his white board shorts were knotted with a small white string. Beyond that she imagined was a fastening. She toyed with the idea of removing his shorts in a playful game of undress but then thought better of it. Too obvious perhaps, she reasoned, for this skillful opposition. He was going to play hard to get. He was going to let her lead the way, just as the ridiculous psychologist had told him to.

She imagined he was as eager as her to begin their intimate relationship. She had felt the heat of his body on hers more than once. She had felt his strong, passionate kisses. She closed her eyes at the memory of his palms on her naked breasts. She wanted nothing more than to be with him. She had thought of nothing more for days now. The wait was killing her.

She wondered about the idea of a game of truth or dare. She imagined that it could ruin the beautiful peace and calm of their surroundings, so she thought better of it. She made a mental note that it would be a good game to play with him later that night.

She remembered the day she awoke to find him running his strong hands over her body in the pretense of applying sun protection cream. Interesting, that could work, except for the fact that she had left it in the cabin.

She had another lovely, delicious memory, of the time when she very nearly made love to her gorgeous friend. She was standing astride him, one leg either side of his torso as she slowly, teasingly removed her underwear.

She recalled the agony on his face as he tried not to rush her, instead taking in every inch of her body and licking his lips in anticipation. His manly arms were held back behind his head in an effort to not grab her and throw her to the bed. Which of course, eventually happened anyway. She now remembered their frantic kissing, his body on hers, her skin burning under his.

She felt certain that they were about to make love for the very first time at that moment. That moment in time a totally unplanned, spontaneous act of pure passion and love. Her body yearned for that feeling once more. Her mind was making her body desperate for his touch.

She needed to feel his hands on her once more. She moved her arm ever so slightly so that their skin was just touching. He felt warm, the sun felt hot, she couldn't wait a moment longer to feel him against her. She only wanted to touch him, for now anyway. She wanted him to feel the hunger she was feeling, the desperation of her need for him. She wanted him to want her. To want her with every ounce of his being but not yet have her.

She glanced again toward him. His body hadn't moved. His face was still and he looked at peace, his eyes closed. How could he be so calm, when she was dying inside with need? She tormented herself with the thought.

She decided to ask him. Try to put herself out of this misery, as she lay beside him feeling undesirable and needy. "Does it feel strange, lying here and not touching me?" Her soft, sexy voice broke through the silence.

He let out a long and exhausted sigh. "You cannot imagine."

She took this as a sign of encouragement and the green light to make her next move. With one seamless and graceful movement, she moved to a sitting position. She inched toward him and placed one long, toned leg over the width of his body to arrive at a sitting position on top of him. Her bottom was sitting lightly on his lap while he remained lying motionless on his back beneath her.

She glanced down at him and bit her lower lip. As if resistance was his best line of defense, he once again, raised his bulging arms and locked his hands together as he placed them behind his head.

For effect, she stayed there, sitting on top of him. Feeling the eagerness of his body rise beneath her. She knew she was having the desired effect.

"If you don't want to touch me, that just means I have to touch myself," she hissed sexily at him.

She lifted both of her small, delicate now manicured hands to the top of her neck. She let her fingers fan out as her hands moved slowly downwards to the base of her neck and then further down to the top of her chest and outwards almost to the edge of her body. She allowed her fingers to gently caress the area beneath them and felt her skin tingle with pleasure at the touch.

She bent her fingers and then extended them out again, moving her hands toward the centre of her body. She brought her hands together, allowing her fingers to entwine slightly as her hands progressed down her body. Her joined fingers found the soft, delicate space between her breasts as they continued moving downward.

Her long fingers gently caressed the sensitive spot as they hesitated, her thumbs lingering behind on this sensual journey to find their way to her soft nipples. Her hands now stopped their slow descent for her thumbs to take their time to gently tease each nipple. As if on command her breasts responded to the feel. Her nipples hardened to the touch as she again bit her lip and playfully threw her head back slowly in ecstasy.

She felt him move beneath her. She could feel his manhood growing with expectation. His tentative and slightly cracked voice broke through the thick air between them.

"What are you trying to do to me?" he begged her for sympathy.

"I want you to touch me," she responded as she released her hands from her body and held out her open palm to him.

It was his turn to bite on his lower lip as he closed his eyelids for a second as if in pure agony. A quiet and low muffled noise rose from his mouth as he lifted his head slightly. He released one arm from its imprisonment to offer up for sacrifice his right hand, palm upturned he placed his hand in hers.

"You give up easily," she toyed with him.

"Easily?" he laughed. "You have no idea, how much pain I am in right now."

"Tell me?" she hissed sexily back at him.

"You are killing me here," he answered her.

As if intent to complete her evil plan, she took hold of his right hand in hers. She turned his palm down onto hers and began to spread his fingers apart. She gently caressed the skin on his hands, looking not at him but focused completely on his strong, masculine hand in hers. She chose his index finger, probably the most sensitive she imagined.

She lifted his large hand and placed it on her left cheek. She held her hand on his, allowing her face to mold into his large palm. She closed her eyes for a second, savouring the touch of his hand on her cheek. She opened her eyes and looked into his face. She couldn't decipher what she read as a mixture of fear and love in his eyes.

She knew he was only trying to protect her but she also knew she needed her lover to come back to her. She lifted his hand from her cheek and held his palm with one hand while she delicately placed his fingers on her lips. She found his index finger and traced her soft moist lips with it. Her eyes caught his. She stared with intent into his now mesmerised face, frozen with anticipation at her next move.

She parted her lips ever so slightly, enough for his finger to move gently inside her mouth. Her tongue found the tip of his finger enough to moisten the hard skin. She allowed her lips to close around his finger for just a moment longer. Her tongue flicked playfully at the tip of his finger. His face was fearful, he looked doubtful that he could survive much more of this torture.

She hoped his control wouldn't last much longer but she had one final test for him. She removed his now moist finger and stared intensely into his eyes. She placed his fingertip on her still hard nipple. He let out a sigh as he began to tease the sensitive skin. His mouth opened as if to speak.

She allowed him full control now as his hand opened and his strong fingers formed a perfect cup around her firm, round breast. She watched as he released his second hand, bringing it quickly to her other breast.

His eyes, not on hers but on her breasts, as with expert movements his hands and fingers caressed, teased and tantalised her soft skin. She once more allowed her head to drop back as she soaked in his every touch. She felt his body begin to move beneath her as if desperate to join hers in every way.

It was as if the ocean, her great love, was written into the script with exact precision. At that precise moment, her mind was brought back to reality by a large splash to the port side of the huge boat. With great excitement she stood up, leaving his hands to drop down on his body having to release the breasts that they had just found.

She stood still for a moment, one leg either side of his body. Standing astride him, she felt his hands now grab each of her legs. His eyes were searching the outline of her entire body as if mesmerised by this beauty before him. She stood silently listening for another clue. It didn't take but a few seconds before she heard it again. A fish and a large sized one at that, jumping through the water.

Seemingly desperate to escape its larger prey, the fish was swimming for its life. Kasie lifted her leg over her lover's body and bent down quickly to grab her discarded top.

She ran toward the boat's rails to look for the offending predator. She gasped as she witnessed a beautiful tiger shark thrashing through the water chasing its next meal.

"Oh," she yelled back at him. "It's a tiger shark, quick!"

Without waiting for a response, Kasie replaced her top as she ran along the narrow path to the back deck of the boat.

Feeling very groggy and not as if he could move with any speed, he made it to his feet slowly. He followed her along the narrow path, holding the rail for support to make it to the back deck in just enough time to see her position her mask over her eyes, place the snorkel in her mouth, her fins having already been expertly applied.

He caught a final glimpse of her tanned body in her white bikini, her long blonde hair catching the wind behind her as she jumped without hesitation into the deep blue water behind the boat. He watched for a second until her head emerged from the surface of the water and she started to paddle, making her way for a close-up encounter with the tiger shark chasing its prey.

He shook his head, smiled a wide, joyful grin and chuckled to himself, "Crazy Aussies!"

SEVEN

THE HEART OF THE OCEAN

Kasie was enjoying her favourite time of the morning in her now preferred part of the boat. She glanced over the bow of the boat and beyond at the clear blue skies around her. As she cupped her hot coffee in her hand, she looked toward the dark blue of the ocean to one side of her and the lighter blue shallower water of the reef to the other.

Such a dichotomy in nature she thought to herself. The deep dark ocean to the right hiding a world of secrets and creatures that preferred to stay hidden in the depths of the ocean. A whole ecosystem surviving, active twenty-four hours a day, constant movement, constant threats happening almost entirely without the watchful eye of the humans who remained firmly on solid ground.

To her other side the reef; the entire reason she came to Coral Cove. The reef which had been her work and her passion for the last three years. Barely hidden in the light blue waters, the reef choosing to expose itself. To allow the world with little effort to see it's beautiful colours and magical creatures. It appeared to invite visitors, onlookers who would marvel at the wonders of the residents, each playing a very important role, dependent on each other for their very survival.

As Kasie looked from side to side, she felt as if the ocean reflected the dichotomy of her own life. Her present represented by the reef; clear, known, friendly and familiar. Her future like the deep dark depths of the ocean floor; unknown, sometimes terrifying, not yet ready to fully expose itself to her. Instead wanting to remain secretive and mysterious.

She wondered if everyone felt like this at some stage in their own lives. Knowing that the present would soon become the past and the future would unravel itself slowly and become the new reality. Having the time alone on the boat, was giving Kasie the opportunity to really think about what her future might look like. She had always imagined going home to Port Douglas. She desperately wanted to see her family and friends who she had virtually neglected for the best part of three years.

She knew her father wasn't happy with her staying away for so long, having promised that she would only live abroad for a year. But she also knew that he would be happy for her doing the work that held so much meaning for her. He loved hearing from her about her adventures; her research and her work on the reef and of course any news about her new friends.

She wondered what he would think if he knew about her latest events, her stalker, Doctor Chris, her two attempted abductions, the drugging, and her possible romance with the town's heir. She didn't dare tell him any of it. She didn't want to worry him. She also didn't want to get his hopes up about her potential romance until she herself understood more about what was actually going on between the two of them.

"Speak of the devil," she laughed as her lover appeared before her, breakfast tray in his hands.

"Where would madam like to dine this morning?" he inquired quite formally.

"Right here, thank you," she giggled back. "This looks amazing." Kasie marveled at the array of food before her. She began immediately to consume the contents of the breakfast tray.

"You sound surprised," he replied as he attempted to feign hurt by her comments.

"Well, it's just that, I didn't know you could cook. I hadn't imagined you ever had to learn," she explained.

"Well, I haven't actually, but Helen has let me dabble in the kitchen on the odd occasion."

The two friends sat and enjoyed their breakfast in the delicious warmth of the morning sun. She couldn't imagine a better place in the world to rest and recuperate. She loved the water and the ocean made her feel an inner peace that few truly understood. She looked toward the blue waters and yearned to once more dive into its warmth, letting the clear liquid engulf her and hold her hostage for a short time, or at least until her oxygen supply ran out.

Free diving had become a recent passion for Kasie. Learning the technique from Marco, she hoped one day to travel to Hawaii to have formal lessons with a well-known free diver and conservationist.

A great new idea began to form in her mind. She imagined how special it would be to have others learn to free dive on this very reef. To learn how to manage your breath and swim for metres under the water without a tank, relying just on your own your lungs, a mask and fins.

It was funny to think of how quickly she had taken to the idea of possibly staying here longer. She didn't dare plan out the next five years of her life but with more and more of her soul, she began to challenge her own beliefs about the ideal of home. The possibilities with what to do to enhance the reef system and bring nature lovers to view its splendour were endless. She wished she had more time to just sit and ponder the numerous options.

"Do we have to go back today?" Kasie asked the question that she didn't really want the answer to.

"Not at all, actually I think another day here is just what we need."

"I am so very glad you said that, because I had an idea. How about we take the tender and head to Long Island to check on the sea grass regeneration. I imagine I am going to have to get a better handle on where it is at with Chris now gone."

He paused. "That sounds like work to me and you haven't been given the all clear to begin work again if you remember correctly."

Kasie knew he was just looking out for her and couldn't help but feel frustrated at the vast number of people who suddenly appeared to have some say in her life. "You know what my Dad would say about that?" she asked him.

"No, but I would love to hear," he replied with genuine sincerity.

"He would say that if you make a living out of doing something you love; you never have to work a day in your life."

"Wise man. I like that," he agreed. "So, am I correct to assume that regardless of what the doctor has instructed you to do, you are going to go to Long Island anyway?"

Kasie smiled at him with a knowing glance, "Now you are beginning to understand."

He smiled back at her as he started to piece together a new theory to explain the motivation behind her actions. "Let me check my understanding of this. If Doctor Phoenix or Doctor Harris told us that we shouldn't engage in any um, how would you say… sexual activity for the next month, until you are fully recovered, you would do the exact opposite?"

"That sounds about right!" Kasie laughed at her own admission.

"Ah," he let out a sigh. "That's going to make my life hell then isn't it?"

Kasie felt confused by this latest confession. "Do you want to explain what you mean by that? I'm not sure I like the sound of that comment," she confessed to him.

He sat thoughtfully for a moment trying to piece together the best explanation for his curious friend. "Kase, I really want to ensure that we do this right and you have time to get better." He paused again and looked into her eyes, his sincerity and concern were obvious to her. "Because I want you and I to be together for a very long time and that means that right now, we have to look after you and let you recover."

"Well, we might have our very first disagreement on our hands then, because you know what I think? I think I am the best judge of what is right for me and if going back to work tomorrow or jumping on your sexy body is right for me, that is exactly what I am going to do!"

He bowed his head in defeat. "You really are going to kill me Kase."

"What do you think then? Are you going to come swimming with turtles at Long Island with me today?" Kasie asked him.

"I don't think I have a choice, do I? Just promise me that you won't overdo it? Ok? Especially after your impromptu shark swim yesterday."

"I promise it won't be all work and no play today."

He smiled as he took in her words. "So, speaking of play, is there anything else you are going to force me to do today?" His face displayed the right combination of hopeful romantic and helpless lover.

"Sounds like you might have a request?" she toyed with him.

"Um, well you know. Whatever I need to do I guess to make you feel better. I am your humble servant." He bowed his head and laughed.

Kasie leant forward and kissed the lips of the man she loved. "Come on, let's eat breakfast and then go for a swim."

Kasie watched as her lover steered the tender carefully through the coral reef of Long Island. A task she imagined he must have performed many times before, having grown up on these islands.

"It's absolutely gorgeous here," she remarked.

"Isn't it?" he agreed.

A round green head breached the surface of the water in front of them.

"That's a good sign," Kasie remarked.

"They must know it's you," her sexy companion added.

They made their way to the beach, pulled the tender up the shore slightly and stood on the hot white sand. Staring back toward the ocean, their massive cruiser looked now like a small toy floating on the blue sea.

"It really is magical, isn't it?" Kasie marveled. "I don't get out here enough, not to do just this."

"We should change that. I could use more days on the ocean. Let's promise that we will do this regularly, just you and me, no staff, no friends, no parties, just you, me, and of course, the turtles and the tiger sharks," he joked.

"That is a promise I can agree to," she smiled back at him.

Without further delay they found their snorkel gear and headed toward the shallow water. They applied their masks and snorkels and finally their fins. Holding her camera in her hand, Kasie looked toward her gorgeous friend.

"Smile!" she said through gritted teeth, the snorkel still in her mouth. Holding the camera in front of them, they both looked towards the lens, the white deserted beach behind them creating the perfect backdrop. They both smiled for the selfie. Turning her attention to the clear, blue water once more, Kasie was the first to plunge in. Her hunky man followed closely behind.

It was only a matter of minutes before the first curious green turtle made his presence known. Swimming by for a playful look at the new arrivals to his island he showed no fear of their presence.

Kasie held her camera out and took the first snapshot. Seeming pleased with the paparazzi attention, the green turtle turned and began swimming around them. Kasie followed closely behind being careful not to touch the marine creature.

The curious turtle swam slowly enough for his new friend to keep up. He swam to the right and then cutting in front of her dodged to the left. Kasie took a breath and swam down to see the turtle more clearly. He looked well, really well. Quite young actually, she guessed. Well-fed and healthy. She swam back to the surface not wanting to put any undue stress on the friendly local.

Swimming into the deeper water, Kasie was pleased to notice the sea grass was growing in thick, dark green clumps in several areas around the island. As insane as Doctor Chris turned out to be, he certainly did a great job at this particular restoration.

Kasie thought she saw a shadow, then another. She saw distinct movement in the darker, deeper water before her. She swam slowly closer to get a better look. A small black tip reef shark darted past her. Then another to the right of her. She raised her head from the water to search for her companion. He wasn't far behind, coming slowly behind her. She paused and replaced her head in the water. She didn't want to do anything to potentially scare these beautiful creatures away.

He finally made his way to her and swam beside her to grab her hand. She pointed in the direction of the curious sharks. She smiled and looked at her companion, mesmerised by the slow, effortless movements of the large shiver of sharks, he watched on intently.

She took his hand and swam slowly, leading him further into the deeper water in an attempt to get a closer look at the black tips. She was curious to see how many there were and overjoyed to see that they had finally made their way back to the reef.

There was a long time when the reef had become quite desolate after the damage of the tsunami. It had taken time for the schools of fish to grow again in population to the vast numbers that existed prior to the enormous wave's arrival.

She felt a squeeze on her hand and heard a soft murmur. He caught her attention and pointed to an enormous manta ray gliding graciously past them and into the dark ocean beyond. She was overjoyed. The number of times she had seen a creature of this size was minimal, maybe two or three times only in her lifetime. She watched as with little effort it disappeared into the distance, just a fleeting second or two watching it as it appeared to fly away silently into the sea.

Kasie could not believe how much she had seen in one small snorkel around the island. She was so excited she barely managed to take many photos at all. She couldn't wait to share her findings with the staff at the research facility. All of these sightings were the most positive signs to date that their hard work had paid off.

By the time Kasie had circled the small island, her partner following closely behind, she was feeling not just relaxed but completely at ease and also very pleased with her findings.

She stopped to chat to her companion, treading water in the deep ocean as she did. "Time to go back to shore maybe?" she asked him.

"Have you seen enough?"

"Yes, it looks great, don't you think?" Kasie answered.

"Gorgeous," he smiled at her.

"Let's swim back to the beach then," Kasie suggested.

They made their way back slowly, enjoying the sights of not only the green turtles but also hundreds of species of colourful fish darting around them. The coral although losing its vibrant colour was somewhat still beautiful in its intricate design and detail. She had a lovely thought to herself as she swam through the warm, clear water, the heat of the sun glowing on her back, I really do have the best job in the world. This same thought had occurred to her time and time again over the last three years. She was so grateful that she had followed her passion and studied marine biology and conservation rather than the more practical courses her parents had tried to lead her into.

And grateful too that somehow she had found and acquired this dream job in this island paradise. She had taken a risk and moved away for a short time in the hope that this particular reef restoration would give her skills and experience far beyond what she could have acquired working back in Australia.

As they approached the shore Kasie stood up on the white sand, careful not to stand on coral or sea grass for fear of damaging it. She removed her mask and snorkel and watched as her friend paddled slowly towards her, still immersed in the beauty of his surroundings. He reached where she was standing and removed his snorkel gear.

"You really have done an amazing thing here," she complimented him.

"I haven't done anything. It is you and your team that has restored this area and the work on the reef," he corrected her.

"And without your money, none of us could afford to do this," she reminded him.

"It's not my money, it was my family's money," he corrected her again.

"Well," she laughed, "I am sure they would be happy to see you putting it to such good use."

They walked through the shallow water until they reached the dry, hot sand once more. Kasie walked up the beach a few steps to sit under the shade of a palm tree. She watched again as the gorgeous, tanned man she was with walked up the beach to join her.

"I hope I am more than just a body to you, I do have a brain and a personality as well," he teased her as he caught her staring at him.

"Oh, really?" she laughed back. "I hadn't noticed. I have a hard time getting past the six pack abs and the biceps."

"Oh, not the tight butt then?" he joked again.

She blushed. "I might have noticed that once or twice before too," she flirted with him.

She felt herself blush as she looked away and glanced once more at the glistening blue water in front of her. The small waves lapped gently on the clear white sand, only broken in places by the smattering of a colourful array of shells in various sizes and shapes.

They looked at the structured pattern the shells created in a curved line to follow the edge of the water. The waves each time forming a line of white foam as it reached its final destination on the shells. Each wave rolled over the shells, sometimes tumbling them over and over until it finally retreated back into the ocean.

Kasie sat and watched, mesmerised with the rhythm of the waves as they repeated their endless dance with the shells time and time again. It was then that she noticed the sparkling green shape in the water. Slightly darker than the other shells and glistening in a way that the others didn't. She stood up and walked toward the shiny object, curious to see what it might be.

She walked down to the water's edge not losing sight for a second of the glistening mystery in front of her.

She bent down and picked up what looked to be a piece of glass. A gorgeous deep emerald green colour, similar she thought to the eyes of her sexy male companion. She turned the glass object over in her hand. She marveled at the sight of this green glass, perfectly shaped by Mother Nature herself into the size and shape of a heart.

She smiled as she remembered the scene from her favourite movie, Billy Zane playing the villain of the piece, the wealthy heir placing a gorgeous blue diamond necklace around the neck of his beloved fiancé, Rose, played by Kate Winslet.

She smiled as she remembered the scene in her head. She spoke softly to herself as she remembered the words of the scene. The necklace, it had a name, it was called… The Heart of The Ocean.

She was startled by the voice beside her. "Has the ocean given you another present?" her companion asked.

"I think so," she responded. "It's, The Heart of The Ocean."

She handed him the perfectly shaped heart. He felt the smoothness of the glass as he moved it between his fingers. "This is amazing," he finally said. "It is a perfect heart shape. It is simply incredible that the ocean could do that."

"You do know about The Heart of The Ocean, don't you?" she questioned him, not quite sure that he had fully understood her reference to her favourite movie of all time.

"Um, no, I don't think so, should I?" he responded with some hesitation.

"Are you serious, it's from my favourite movie… Titanic. You haven't ever seen it?"

"I guess not," he shrugged. "But I have a feeling I am about to in the not too distant future," he added with a chuckle.

"I cannot believe I didn't know that about you. How have we never watched Titanic together?" She paused to hatch a new plan. "Tonight!" she said excitedly, "Let's download it tonight and watch it after dinner."

She glanced once more at the heart in his hand. "Maybe we should leave it here," she suggested. "It belongs to the sea."

"No, we should keep it. I think it is a present for you from the sea," he replied back quickly as he carefully tucked the precious find into his back pocket.

EIGHT

THE DARE

Later that night as Kasie promised, the two friends sat in their familiar position beside each other on the lounge aboard the luxury cruiser as they watched the movie, Titanic. Kasie cuddled up next to her friend and snuggled in for warmth on the slightly chilly night on the water. She watched his face as he stared at the screen.

The closing scenes of her favourite movie played out for them. She watched the screen then turned to explore his face as the elderly female actress playing the lead character, Rose in the movie climbed onto the huge rails of the ship. She held out her hand and with a small squeal, threw the massive blue diamond necklace into the ocean.

They continued their viewing, the elegant necklace sinking quickly into the far deaths of the deep sea never to be seen again. He watched the screen as the young stars of the movie met once more by the clock tower of the enormous luxury cruise liner. Their travelling companions standing around to support the long-lost lovers finding each other again. As the credits rolled he turned to see her staring at him obviously looking for a reaction.

"Well?" she prompted him almost immediately. "What did you think?"

"It was sad."

"But beautiful though," she prompted him again to elicit the response she was actually hoping for.

"But I don't get it, why did she have to throw the necklace in the water. Why didn't she want to give it to her granddaughter?" he asked with a tone of confusion in his voice.

"Well, it's like she said, a woman's heart is as deep as the ocean. And her heart always belonged to Jack. I guess she was returning her heart to where they were last together."

He still looked confused, or displeased. She couldn't quite work out which one. She was a little disappointed that he appeared so caught up on the smaller details rather than seeing the movie for the amazing love story that it was. She wondered if he was truly the hopeless romantic she had thought, or maybe hoped he was.

He continued. It appeared that he had more than a couple of questions about the plot of the three-hour long love story. "But if Rose had managed to move slightly to the side, Jack could have joined her on the floating door and they both could have lived."

Kasie let out a huge sigh. She had spent years debating this particular issue with friends. Photos of how the two lovers could have actually made it work featured on social media posts. People all over the world debated how both could have lived if only Jack had managed to fit on the door as well.

"Seriously though!" she responded. "Is that all you are taking away from the movie?"

"Well I guess I am wondering if she always loved Jack, why did she marry and begin a family with someone else?"

"Ah! Men!" Kasie was beyond frustrated with all the questions. She just wanted him to enjoy the love story without all the inane questions. She decided she would give up before he had another chance to ask anything more.

"Truth or dare?" She changed the topic abruptly, remembering her idea of a playful game with her lover.

He smiled and chuckled. "I don't know if that is a good idea. I have a feeling that I might not enjoy this game."

"Truth or dare?" she asked again, not ready to surrender to his protests.

He smiled at her and turned his head to the side and with a sweet innocence as his eyes pleaded with her to end this torment. He knew he would be playing with fire if he took her up on her offer.

"Don't make me ask again," she spoke more sternly this time.

He sighed and bowed his head. There was no compromise in her voice. "Ok, truth."

She didn't have to think long for a question. She had one formulating in her head as they had watched the movie together. "Have you ever loved anyone like Jack loved Rose?" She was of course referring to the movie and the epic love story between the two characters. The question was a good one.

"Is this a trick question?" he smiled back at her.

"No, it's your question and you have to answer truthfully!" she reminded him of the game rules.

"Well…" he started before pausing to carefully choose his words, "There was this insane Aussie girl this one time. You might know her…" he joked with his companion.

"Seriously!" she interrupted him, "You need to answer this seriously."

"I am serious Kase. I love you as Jack loves Rose… more even."

"What about before me?" she hesitantly asked, but not really wanting to know any more than what he had already admitted to.

His tone was now serious, his voice deep as he answered her question with all honesty. "No… no one before you." He paused and looked at her face to ensure that the answer was acceptable to her.

She took in the enormity of what she had just heard. She was his first love. Just as he was hers! She couldn't have imagined it possible, being the age they were, she had just assumed somehow that she was the unlucky one in love and that everyone around her had already met and fallen in love at least once. But here she was, with a man who was being undeniably honest with her in telling her that she was his first love. Kasie felt a shiver up her arms at the thought of what she had just heard.

"Now you Kase, your turn. Truth or dare?"

"Um… dare I think?" Kasie replied with some hesitancy.

"I was hoping you would say that." The wicked glint in his eyes clued her in to what was in store for her. It didn't take long for him to formulate his dare and offer his instructions. "Ok, you have to kiss me for three minutes straight, without stopping," he instructed her.

"Seriously, that's easy!" She laughed at how simple that would be. She stood to begin her task, pleased that it wasn't more difficult.

He stood to meet her, placing his hands on her hips to stop her in her place and complete the instructions. "Three minutes straight and without touching any part of me beside my lips."

She tilted her head as if to process the added instruction. She should have guessed it wouldn't have been that simple. Not with this man. Not with her friend. Nothing he ever did was easy. "Can you touch me?" she asked him.

"Of course!" He paused and for added effect included yet more detailed rules, "I can touch you anywhere I like." He smirked a wild, sexy grin at her. She knew she was in trouble.

Kasie smiled at the thought. "That seems a little unfair," she demanded.

"It's your game remember! You started this and those are my rules. If you need to forfeit I understand but that means I have won."

She looked into his sexy eyes. They lit up every time he played with her like this. He acted innocent and sweet most of the time, but she had begun to know this sexier side to him. The pure passion and sex appeal of this guy was through the roof. She loved a good challenge. She reached out to the phone on the table next to her, found the stopwatch and activated a timer at three minutes. "Just so you don't cheat," she smiled at him.

"Ok ready?" she asked him.

He smiled back at her, not needing to answer verbally. They both knew he was more than ready to begin the torture he had quickly conjured up in his mind.

Her kiss began gently. She teased his closed lips slowly, her lips only slightly apart and a little moist. She flirted with a gentle caress of her lips on his. His hands were on her as he promised they would be. First on her hips and then on the small of her back pushing her firmly but gently against his hard body.

She held her hands behind her back, clasping them together at the fingers so as not to be tempted to break the rules of the game.

His hands moved down her back and cupped the perfectly round, firm cheeks of her bottom before pushing her further and harder into his body. Her eyes flitted open to see his eyes staring directly into hers, the side of his perfect mouth now upturned into what she imagined was a cheeky grin. His eyes were smiling at her. He lifted his left hand and placed his palm over her eyelids indicating for her to close them again.

His lips began to part more, kissing her harder in return. She felt her passion match his and her lips became frantic to meet his. With paced and exact precision, slowly and gently he began to run his two hands up the sides of her body. Gently tracing the curve of her waistline beneath the thin fabric of her dress. She felt her body tingle with excitement as his hands were approaching that ticklish, sensitive area near the outside of the edge of her breasts. She forced her eyes closed and suppressed her desire to giggle as his fingers touched the sensitive skin.

That's cheating, she thought to herself but couldn't say out loud. Knowing that he had found her sensitive spot before, she didn't think it was sporting to take advantage of her in this way. His hands moved away. Just in time, she thought, she didn't know how much more of that torture she could stand.

She slowed her kisses to a steadier pace. She wanted to remain in control of this game. She wondered how long it had been already. It was impossible to tell. Her fear spiked again as she felt his large hands find her breasts. She held her breath in anticipation of what was to come. She clenched her fingers more tightly behind her. His hands found her soft, warm breasts, his fingers wasting no time to locate her now hard nipples beneath the sheer fabric.

His fingers teased her hard nipples as his tongue pushed past her lips to find hers. Her palms now beginning to feel moist with anticipation were forcing her fingers to slip apart. As if sensing her weakness, his hands travelled to her shoulders, his fingers finding the shoestring strap of her dress and wasting no time, he slowly slipped the dress off her shoulders to reveal her now naked breasts in front of him.

As if pleased with himself, she once again felt his mouth move to form the shape of a smile as his kissing momentarily paused. His hands moved now down towards the unprotected and exposed skin of the hard, pink nipples and the soft, white flesh of her round breasts. His palms and fingers outstretched gently cupped her breasts until his fingers again found their favourite toy, her responsive, reactive nipples.

Her body was tingling from the top of her head to the very end of her toes. She felt a knot in her stomach and an ache in her groin. She felt her body respond to his touch. She moved her body closer to his, pressing herself further and harder against him. The feeling was pure pain, pure ecstasy.

She wouldn't last much longer. She didn't think she would ever hear the timer on her phone sound, allowing her to finally extract herself from this agony. She released her hands and dropped them to her side, allowing her dress to now fall to the ground, exposing just the small white lace G-string she was wearing. She wrapped her arms around his waist and without delay began to find his hot skin beneath his shirt.

He froze and immediately pulled his lips from hers. He looked her in the eyes, as his hands found hers on his stomach. As he removed her hands from his body he returned them to behind her back, holding them in place for just a second as he whispered in her ear.

"You cheated. You are not allowed to touch me. Now you have to start the three minutes all over again."

NINE

THE SHOWER

The game of the night before caused Kasie a night of restless sleep as her companion insisted that yet again, they spend the night apart in order for her to rest. The sexual frustration she was feeling was unbearable. She had tossed and turned unable to get to sleep as visions of his hands on her body played out in her mind. She didn't know how much longer she could last without making love to him. If that was indeed what they decided they were going to do.

She had enjoyed a shower to re-energise and breakfast one last time on the deck before she joined her captain to motor back to the harbour.

They watched the land materialise before them. Today was the day they returned home, to the reality of their daily lives. Also, to their friends waiting eagerly for their return to the mainland.

"I want to go home. I really do, but I don't want to leave the reef yet," Kasie confessed to him.

He placed a comforting arm around her while keeping an eye on his course and his other hand firmly on the boat's shiny, silver wheel.

"We will go out again soon, I promise and next time will be even better." He glanced toward her with a smile on his face. "Next time, you will be fully recovered and we can spend more time actually in the boat."

"Ah!" The disapproving sound escaped from her lips. "I don't understand why you refuse to believe me when I tell you that I am better. There is no need for all this waiting. I swear, if you don't make love to me soon, I promise I will return to Australia."

He laughed at her empty threat. "As if I would let you! Kase, I'm not letting you go anywhere for a very long time." He paused before continuing with an explanation. "I just want our first time to be special, not rushed. And we had fun last night, didn't we?"

Her face went crimson at the thought of his erotic tease of the night before. Her having to hold her hands behind her back, her lips on his while he was able to molest her naked body. "Not exactly fun for me," she replied.

"More like torture."

"Really?" His tone questioned her. "You seemed to enjoy it."

"Sometimes," she continued, "I think you are a hopeless romantic and then sometimes I think you are an evil tormentor."

"Ha!" he laughed, not needing to answer. He knew that Kasie enjoyed the teasing as much as he did. But if he had to admit it, the sexual frustration he was feeling was unbearable. He felt some relief that Kasie was at least feeling it too.

They pulled into the busy harbour as Marco and James came into view. Both men positioned on standby along with the harbour staff, at the ready to assist with mooring the huge vessel. Marco was the first onboard, rushing toward Kasie, arms outstretched. "You've returned safely!" He seemed overjoyed as he enveloped her in one of his familiar strong hugs.

"Well barely actually." She frowned as she motioned toward her sexy companion.

Marco positioned himself between the two lovers, placing a protective arm around Kasie's shoulders as he walked her toward the inside of the boat. "Come on Kasie, tell Marco all about it."

"I can't find the words Marco, it was really that bad!" Kasie jested as she glanced back at her friend, making sure he was listening to her dreadful acting performance. "But enough of me, how's Dee? What's happening with you two then?" she questioned Marco.

"Well unlike others, Kasie." He too, glanced back at his friend for maximum impact, "I don't kiss and tell."

"Oh, so there has been kissing has there?" Kasie pried even further. "You know she will tell me. Us girls tell each other everything." She smiled as she glanced back one final time to see her lover standing motionless in place listening to their humorous dialogue with a wry smile on his face.

The trio travelled back to the house in Marco's car, leaving James at the Harbour to oversee the staff working on mooring and securing the vessel.

Kasie entered the Mansion's huge wooden and glass door and began her travel through the grand entry heading out in search for Dee. She didn't need to go far, as Dee heard the procession of people entering the house and guessed her friend had arrived home. The women saw each other and like long lost lovers, ran toward each other, arms outstretched.

"What took you so long, Kasie?" Dee challenged her immediately as she saw her.

The two men walked through the front door, just in time to hear Kasie's reply to her best friend. "Come upstairs I will tell you all about it."

Marco looked toward his boss. "This is going to be trouble."

Without needing to respond with words, his boss just shook his head in agreement.

"Given your obvious concern, do I need to ask what you have been up to?" his boss asked Marco.

"Yeah, best you don't ask, I think." Marco turned and walked toward the staircase, arms full of Kasie's luggage.

"Should I put these in the master bedroom Kasie?" Marco asked his friend as he ascended to the top of the staircase only seconds after the two girls.

"Oh, I'm sorry Marco, I should have said. I left them in the car on purpose. I am just going to pack up the rest before I head home."

"What?" Dee yelled at her. "Home? Home where?"

"Home to my little house of course, you are coming with me, aren't you Dee?"

Dee looked toward Marco and then back to her friend. "Well, I guess if I have to. I was kind of quite settled here in the mansion though, you know."

"Does he know?" Marco asked Kasie quietly aware that his boss was just beneath them on the ground floor.

"I am sure you are about to tell him," Kasie replied with a firm, determined tone.

"Great... this again." Marco dropped the bags in the hallway of the first floor and made his way back down the stairs to sort out the latest drama.

Kasie and Dee now safely behind closed doors in Kasie's guest room were barely able to contain their excitement at sharing with their best friend all the news of the last few days.

It was Dee's turn to begin. She shared the journey back to Coral Cove aboard The Kingdom. An unconscious Doctor Chris on the boat, only waking in time to see the vessel pulling into the wharf. The excitement as police met Marco and his security team at the harbour and immediately handcuffed the scientist to escort Chris Bartlett to jail to await trial.

Following their heroic adventure, Dee and Marco decided that they both deserved a night off and a few cocktails at The Gaol. Dee described the jubilation of the night. Her sharing the news with the concerned crowd that Kasie had been found safe and well and Chris had been arrested. Everyone wanted to buy her and Marco drinks as they danced the night away. "And then," Dee continued, "Marco and I, we… um… we…" Dee was hesitant to finish her sentence.

"Oh my god, don't tell me everyone in this town is having sex besides me?" Kasie finished her friend's sentence for her with pure frustration.

"Ouch" Dee responded. "Still not?"

"No Dee! And it is absolutely killing me!"

"But why?" Dee asked with empathy and sensitivity.

"That ridiculous Doctor Phoenix. He convinced our friend that I was suffering from trauma and not ready to get involved with him just yet. He must have made him promise to take it slow and not rush me into anything including sex."

"Ow!" was all Dee could manage. "That must be um, hard. Sorry for the poor choice of words."

"I swear I can't stand it Dee. This guy is so sexy and he teases me relentlessly. I am about to explode."

"Is that why you want to go back to your house?"

"Partly, but mainly because it is just that, my house. I don't actually live here in the mansion you know. I have just been a temporary guest while I recovered. I am feeling much better and want to go home."

Dee looked at her friend and tried to comprehend everything she had been through and now this. She secretly wondered if there was more to this than just following the doctor's orders. She hoped not for Kasie's sake. "Ok, well, why don't we start packing here and then we can pack up my room and head home." Dee paused for a moment, then got a great idea. "How about tonight at home, we order pizza and watch some cheesy reality television?"

"Sounds perfect," Kasie agreed, happy to have a night of normalcy with her best friend. "I will go and grab a few things I left in his room while you start here. I won't be a minute."

Kasie left her friend to begin her task as she headed for the door.

Kasie knocked on the door as she arrived at the master bedroom. Unsure whether he was actually in his room or not, she thought it would be best to just make him aware of her presence in case he was in the middle of something. No response. She knocked a second time. Pressing her ear against the large, thick wooden door, she heard nothing. She grabbed the door handle, turned and opened the large door to his room.

She had only walked a few steps inside the room when she heard the noise. The familiar sound of his shower running in his bathroom. She now understood why he didn't respond to her knocking. She made her way to the bedside table where she found a few items of her clothing, discarded and left after the steamy session with the master bedroom's resident.

She recalled the events to herself. The thought of the passion she shared with this man and the constant rejections lately. She felt certain she was deserving of it, given that she fended off his advances when he first professed his love for her. But being that it was now her at the centre of the rejection, it felt completely different.

She turned to glance at the closed bathroom door, the sound of the shower still radiating into the room. The image she pictured in her head of the stunning man standing naked, lathering up a foaming wash and running it over his body. Kasie smiled to herself and without waiting another second, removed her dress, her bra and her panties.

Checking herself quickly in the mirror, she was pleased with what she saw. She made her way to the bathroom door and turned the handle.

Blissfully unaware of the guest approaching the shower door, he was caught in his own thoughts. He didn't hear his friend sneak into the room, nor pry open the steamy shower door. He didn't sense her enter the hot, wet shower cubicle until he felt her soft, gentle hands on his manhood.

Kasie had waited until his back was turned, she opened the shower door and without a second's delay wrapped her slight arms around him and placed her hands directly on his naked penis. He stood still, seemingly unconcerned with the surprise guest in his shower. He let his head fall back as her hands began to masterfully pleasure him. He had longed for the touch of her hands on him. His body has been aching to feel her, to be close to her, to be inside of her.

He reached down and placed his hands on hers, peeling them off his body he held them tightly. He turned around to face his now wet, naked friend. Gently but forcefully he moved her body until she was trapped against the steamy glass wall of the shower. He pressed his body hard against hers as his lips once again found hers. He kissed her passionately, still holding her hands.

Restraining her hands in his, he began to move her arms as he placed them hard against the glass and high above her head. He held her in place, frantically kissing her lips. He slowly moved his head down to kiss her neck, then her chest, finally stopping at her breast as his tongue flicked her once again erect nipple.

He allowed her hands to drop and felt them around him once more. He could hear her steady but hard breath over the sound of the pounding water. He flicked her nipple once, this time his hand firmly cupping her breast. His head moved to her other breast, finding that sweet, sensitive spot that made her groan with pleasure.

He listened to her moan with agony at his touch. He released her breast from his warm mouth and found her face once again. He kissed her lips just once and found her ear. "Maybe you need a little something to take the edge off," he smiled at his own suggestion.

Without waiting for a response, he bent his knees slightly. His mouth beginning to trace her body as it moved slowly past her neck, over her breast, down her stomach, stopping only when it reached its destination between her legs. She moaned once more as he began to kiss her. Her open palms now clutching at the slippery, wet glass of the shower.

She struggled to remain standing as he worked his magic on her sensitive and sensual body.

She screamed out in joy.

He smiled again to himself as he enjoyed hearing for the first time ever what he thought was the most sensual sound he had ever heard.

TEN

THE MOVIE NIGHT

"Suddenly decided that you needed a shower?" Dee laughed at her friend as Kasie finally returned to her guest room.

"Um, yes I guess," Kasie stammered.

"Well, I have packed your room and mine, we are ready to go. That is if you still want to." Dee was hopeful that Kasie might have suddenly changed her mind and that they both might be staying in the luxurious mansion for a while longer.

"No, I want to go home, at least for now. Are you ready to leave?" Kasie asked her friend.

"Not really. I have got quite settled here but if you insist. Let's go then," Dee agreed very reluctantly.

Walking back into her home was harder than she had imagined it would be. Her memory of Chris threatening her life and the life of her friend was still fresh in her mind.

Noticing her friend's hesitation as she entered through the front door, Dee asked, "Are you ok Kasie?"

"It just feels a little strange, you know. It doesn't feel the same anymore." She stopped and looked around the small house. "So much has happened, this being my safe, comfortable little house, feels like a lifetime ago."

"Well, it is, sort of. Since you last lived here you now are virtually engaged, you are about to take over management of the research facility and the conservation society and you have your best friend back in your life." Dee smiled at her in a direct attempt to lighten her mood.

"Yes, I guess you are right, except for the engagement part," she added. "We are not engaged, not even close. We are simply friends still at the moment."

"Wow, when did that change? I mean I don't know too many friends that find themselves showering together." Dee looked at Kasie with a grin from ear to ear.

Kasie knew she wasn't able to defend herself with any real substance and merely smiled back at Dee.

"Ok, let's execute this plan," Dee began excitedly. "I will begin some downloads, while you order the pizzas. Oh, and I have a little present here from Marco." She reached into her bag and pulled out a chilled bottle of vodka.

Kasie smiled at her. "And I am hoping that by about the middle of that bottle, you might start spilling the gossip on your little fling thing."

"Maybe, just maybe, if you are lucky," Dee teased a little more with her friend.

The night progressed without drama which was fortunate as it allowed Kasie to begin to feel a bit more relaxed in her own home again. Fueled by a few vodka cocktails, cheesy reality television and good food, Kasie was stretched out on her comfortable blue and white couch.

"So, tell?" She began to push Dee again for information on her and Marco.

"What's there to tell?" Dee wasn't giving much away even with the added incentive of alcohol to loosen her lips.

"Are you in love?" Kasie emphasised the last word for effect.

"I wouldn't say that but Marco is a lot of fun."

"Yeah, so I hear," Kasie added. "You're not the first girl to describe Marco as a lot of fun, or a great kisser or amazing in the bedroom."

"Yes, he is all that." Dee looked skywards at the memory. "But is he really as much of a player as they say?"

"Well Marco has always been one of those guys that lives by the motto, play hard, work hard and he has been working hard while working on the search and rescue team so maybe he is just making up for lost time." Kasie giggled a little. "But I must admit, since you have been around, I haven't ever seen him so attentive. Maybe you have changed him."

"No thanks. I am not trying to change anyone. We were just having a little fun. A bit of a holiday romance maybe." Dee's tone was thoughtful.

Her mood changed somewhat as she added the next piece of information. "A holiday that is, that really has to end sometime in the very near future."

"No Dee," please don't say that. I can't bear the thought of you not being here in all this craziness with me.

"Well, I have a job to get back to, you know."

"You could work here with me?" Kasie responded hopefully. "And beside that I need you here while I work through this trauma that I apparently have."

Dee looked at her in all seriousness now and asked, "Are you admitting that you might need some support to get past all of this?"

"Um, depends on what kind of support. If you are suggesting me talking to Doctor (I know everything) Phoenix then I don't think so."

Dee amped up the seriousness, "Well maybe he is a good starting point. Maybe if you chatted to him, he might refer you to someone more to your liking perhaps?"

"Maybe, I'll think about it." Was all Kasie was prepared to commit to.

"So, let's change the subject, what are we watching next?" Kasie asked. "Do you want to watch Titanic?"

"Oh god no. We have seen that a hundred times already," Dee protested.

"A hundred and one now," Kasie corrected her. "We watched it on the boat together."

"Kasie, that man truly loves you! If he sat and watched that tripe with you for three hours, he truly loves you. Don't let him go!"

Her first night back in her own bed was a restless one. Despite a few vodkas in an attempt to help her sleep, Kasie couldn't quite feel comfortable in her own space. When she closed her eyes, the image of Doctor Chris walking into her room popped into her head. Despite doing everything she could think of to recall more pleasant memories, her mind kept taking her back to that horrible day of her abduction. She considered the possibility that she did indeed need to talk to someone. It couldn't hurt, she imagined.

Kasie was awake early, dressed and ready for her first day back at work. She scribbled Dee a note as she finished her coffee. Doing a final check in the mirror before she walked out the door, Kasie paused to look at the woman in front of her. She was performing all her normal tasks this morning, going about getting showered, dressed, applying her makeup, grabbing a piece of toast and coffee before work, but none of it felt the same. She looked the same, same hair, same eyes, a slightly darker tan given her few days on the boat, but she didn't feel the same person anymore.

She knew she felt slightly less sexually frustrated given her shared shower of the day before, but there was more to it than that. It felt as if she was walking around through a strange dream, as if none of what was going on around her was real anymore.

She wondered if the lack of sleep was making her feel this way, slightly disconnected from everything around her. She made a mental note to ring Doctor Phoenix for an appointment. He seemed to have the answers to everything, so he thought, so why not see if he could shed some light on what had been happening to her.

Possibly more time was all she needed. There had been a lot happen to her in a very short time but being the way that she was, she didn't want to dwell. Maybe she just needed a few days of normality to feel like herself again.

As she made her way into the car park at the research facility she thought she was going to be one of the first to arrive. The car park was almost at capacity and it was only eight o'clock. She made her way to the entry where she was greeted by the smiling Rachel, on reception.

"Good morning Kasie." Rachel greeted her. "I didn't know you were back today. Are you here for the big meeting?"

"Um, no. It was a last-minute decision to return today. What meeting?"

"Our funder, you know the big man who pays all our bills. He has called a meeting today at nine o'clock." Rachel added in explanation.

"Oh, I better get some information put together for him then." Kasie tried to look professional, but inside her stomach tied itself into knots imagining her lover here at her office within the hour.

"Um, and you will need this." Rachel added as she held out a round swipe tag the size of a small coin. "We have new security too, so you will need this to access your office. I believe yours has full access of the building. Lucky you!"

"Yes, lucky me," Kasie parroted, not trying to sound sarcastic but simply trying to make sense of these rapid changes in her workplace.

Having made it to her office without further delay, Kasie was pleased that she hadn't passed anyone else in the hallway. She wanted to make it to her office, close her door and take a deep breath. She needed a minute to calm herself in preparation for his arrival. She sat at her desk and searched her bag for the memory card from her camera. As she placed the card into the small slot on her laptop, the photos immediately began to display. Photos of the sea grass and of the green turtle happily posing for her.

She looked at the photos of the ocean from the beach and the hundreds of colourful fish on the reef. And then, she saw it, the photo of the two of them. Looking like two love-struck kids, snorkel and mask in place on their face, their heads pushed together to fit into the camera lens as Kasie took the selfie.

She hovered over the photo. Her skin began to tingle and her face felt warm as she stared at the image. This man had the same effect on her even in photographic form. She really was a hopeless case as far as he was concerned. Did she have no self-control left whatsoever? She glanced at the clock. Time was ticking away and she was feeling less in control than when she had first arrived.

She continued to import the bright, colourful images of her day at Long Island onto the laptop. Carefully choosing the right ones to share, she uploaded some onto a power point presentation along with some interesting stats. At least, she thought to herself, I will have something worthwhile to add to the meeting. And, she added a mental note to herself and if nothing else, it looked as if she had actually been doing some work.

She gathered her things and began to make her way to the door. Checking the time again, she figured she had fifteen minutes before the meeting started to make herself another coffee and check her make up in the mirror. She suddenly realised she had left the security tag behind. She walked back to her desk and was intently rummaging through her bag looking for the small black tag. She was so invested in the search she didn't hear the door open and close behind her.

She didn't hear his quiet, soft footsteps. The first sign that he was here was his strong, warm hand on her side, resting gently on her hip, his other hand pulling back her long blonde hair from her neck as his warm, moist lips made contact with the sensitive skin on her neck. She closed her eyes at the touch, her body and mind unable or unwilling to fight it.

"I didn't expect to see you here," he said as he finally spoke. His mouth paused close enough to her ear for his warm breath to send shivers down her spine.

"I decided to come in and check on things," she replied, barely able to get the words out as the spell of his touch worked its way through her body and now to her almost incoherent brain.

"I am glad to see you here. Have I ever told you how sexy you look in your office attire?"

She turned to face him, pinned between him and the edge of her desk she was barely able to turn around. She tried to sound indignant. "No and you know why you have never said that?" She paused for just a second, not really waiting for a response. "Because it would be totally inappropriate for you to do that, seeing as you are my boss."

Failing to notice her warning, instead appearing more turned on than chastised, he flashed his wide, flirty smile at her. "Want to make love to your boss on your desk then?"

As her knees went weak and she felt as if she could collapse into his arms, she surprisingly found enough inner strength to raise her two palms against his chest and give him a playful push. "That is totally inappropriate behaviour in the workplace." She couldn't help but grin as she flirted with him. His strong torso pushed past the force of her hands against him.

He leant forward once more. His mouth was nearly touching hers, his whole body now pressing firmly against her, pushing her hard against the edge of the table. "How about another shower then?" he laughed a little as his huge smile lit up his face.

She laughed with him. His sex appeal was incredible. Dropping the pretense of professionalism, she replied with a smile. "Maybe later?"

He kissed her lips and then before she realised what had happened, he had turned and left the room.

Despite a nervousness, the like of which she hadn't felt in years, she managed to make it through the meeting. It was more pleasantries than business really. The man running the meeting, updating the staff on the charges against Doctor Chris, on their job security and on their new Managing Director. He paused the speeches for a moment at that point, enough time for the staff to applaud the welcome announcement.

Not being able to resist the opportunity for a little fun at her expense, he insisted she stand, while her staff showed their appreciation of her safe return and her commitment to continue the important work following Chris's departure.

She warmly greeted each of the staff, thanking them for their show of support. She looked at each person in the room, making eye contact and mouthing the words thank you to each of them. She finally stopped at the man in the front of the room. Standing there leading the applause, his wide smile and bright eyes, a convincing cover for a man seen to be merely appreciative of the efforts of a senior staff member.

Only she could see behind the façade of this very professional looking man and saw the real intent of her boss standing before her, scanning her body up and down, possibly imagining her again naked in the shower.

At the conclusion of the meeting, they waited for the staff to vacate the large boardroom before they spoke. James the last to leave sensed that a private conversation between his boss and the new Managing Director was in order. He closed the door behind himself as he left the room.

"That went well," Kasie started.

"I wanted to keep everyone informed," he began by way of explanation.

"Can I walk you out?" she asked, keen to remove this very real threat to her professionalism from the building.

"Keen to get rid of me?" he questioned her intentions, his face fallen into the shape of a frown.

"Rather keen to get some work done, boss," she explained.

As they walked down the hall together making their way to the entrance of the building they were stopped by a very excited Aretha. "That is great news Kasie." She directed the comment to her manager, "Does that mean you are staying in Coral Cove permanently?" she added hopefully.

Feeling extremely awkward at not having an answer readily prepared for the inevitable questions, Kasie glanced toward her boss for a helpful interjection. He simply smiled back at her, raising his eyebrows as if he too was looking forward to hearing her reply.

"Um, it's a little complicated at the moment Aretha. I can't say that I have made a decisive decision one hundred percent either way, at the moment, but I will let you know when I know. Is that ok?" Kasie added, hoping that she had given enough of an answer to satisfy the young intern.

His strong male voice began as hers trailed off. "Let's just say, Aretha. I am in negotiations at the moment to try to keep Kasie here permanently." He smiled as he looked firstly at Aretha and then back to Kasie. As he looked directly into Kasie's eyes, his tone softened as he added "And I am feeling confident, we are close to a suitable agreement."

Not sensing the undercurrent at all, Aretha appeared satisfied with the response, "Well that's great. I will let Annie know. She wanted to ask as well." With that the young woman disappeared as quickly as she appeared before them.

The two friends continued to walk down the hallway, through the reception and past the front door and into the car park as they talked.

"Am I to understand that your interns don't know about The List?" he asked her.

"They are a little young to be socialising at The Gaol, so they might not be up on all the juicy gossip of Coral Cove."

"Well it might come as some surprise to them when we announce our engagement."

"What?" Kasie stopped in her tracks, not expecting those few words to be uttered at this present moment.

"I hope you haven't forgotten that I asked you to marry me," he began, getting straight to the point in suddenly a very businesslike fashion.

"And I didn't exactly say yes, if you remember correctly." She paused to see him take in that information. "And beside that, I thought you were under instructions to take it easy, no talk of marriage or children while I recover? She raised her fingers in the way of exclamation marks around the last word.

He considered his words carefully before replying to her. "I am not normally a patient man and it is killing me trying to take this slowly, but don't confuse that with me not wanting to quickly make you my wife." He looked hopefully into her eyes.

She bowed her head but said nothing.

"Kase." He placed his hand under her chin to raise her eyes to his. "Are you ok?"

She didn't reply.

Still looking at her sad eyes he continued. "Kase, I know we have to wait, but I think we should make the announcement as soon as we can. It's only fair."

Kasie knew he was correct. She also knew she wanted this man in her life more than she had wanted anything before.

She just didn't know what this growing hesitation was within her to begin this amazing new life with him. "I know. Me too. It's only right to be honest. I don't want to feel like we have to hide this. It's just I'm not ready right now, not yet."

"I know." His gentle eyes were still searching hers. "I am trying to be patient, to take it slow." He paused and brought his lips to her ear. "It is killing me you know. I may have mentioned this to you already." He returned his eye contact with hers.

"Me too," she simply replied.

He began to walk to the car. As if trying to establish some form of professionalism he didn't kiss her goodbye. She watched him walk away. She could just make out the outline of his tight rear in his business pants as he headed to the car.

"Oh," he stopped and turned towards her once more. "I thought a party was in order, hope you are free Saturday night?"

She nodded back at him.

"At the mansion, as you like to call it," he added. He smiled at her, lowered his voice somewhat as he added his final few last words before entering the car, "Oh, and sleepovers are on offer!"

Kasie watched the car drive off, made her way back to her office, and immediately closed the door behind her. She reached for the phone and dialed. "Hello, yes, I would like to make an appointment with Doctor Phoenix please."

She paused as she listened to the voice on the other end of the phone.

"Yes, Kasie McCarthy. Tomorrow, that's perfect. See you then."

ELEVEN

THE SESSION

Kasie had been waiting patiently but nervously in the office of Doctor Phoenix. Having been let in by his reception staff, she sat down on the brown leather couch and scanned the walls of the office. Degree after degree, framed and in date order, lined the painted walls. Never feeling the need to talk to a psychologist before, Kasie wasn't sure she knew exactly how to start.

She had spoken to the psychologist on several occasions already. The most recent being just a few weeks ago when she told him she wanted to take her name off The List. She remembered his seemingly inappropriate comment about her attire as if challenging her on whether her intentions on that night were innocent or not. She remembered thinking how rude he was to suggest that she wore something considered inappropriate on the night she planned to talk to the bachelor about her long-term plans, which did not include him.

She remembered the psychologist accepting her explanation of why she wanted to take her name off The List but then still attempting to get her to reconsider. She wondered now, thinking back to that strange night, how much he actually knew of his client's long-term plans. Asking her to reconsider her decision to take her name off

The List, she wondered if his client had actually been talking to him long before he professed his love directly to Kasie.

Of course, she thought to herself, now knowing that the psychologist was a trusted confidant to her lover. She now understood his reaction. Her curiousity grew as she wondered how much more he actually knew about their friendship and developing relationship.

A slight knock on the door and Doctor Phoenix appeared. All smiles, he greeted her with a handshake. "Good morning Kasie, it is lovely to see you today and especially looking so well. What can I do for you this morning?"

Kasie paused not quite knowing where to start. "Well first thing is, I am furious at you telling him to take it easy and some ridiculous talk of me having trauma. I want you to stay out of our relationship."

"The two of you are in a relationship then?" The Doctor immediately honed in on the one word she didn't mean to say.

"That is irrelevant," she angrily replied, crossing her arms in the process.

"Is it?" the doctor challenged further, "I thought that was precisely the reason for your visit."

"Well it appears that you know more than me yet again. I don't even know why I am here," she retorted.

The Doctor continued, "Maybe it is just that I am more willing to discuss the reason behind your visit and you are still not ready to name it."

"So, continue Doctor, why am I here?"

"I am hoping you can tell me Kasie, but I would guess it has something to do with what we call trauma."

Kasie sat listening but not yet ready to intervene.

"Can I ask Kasie, are you having trouble sleeping? Or having flashbacks or memories of what has happened to you? Are you having any physical symptoms, stomach aches, nausea, anything unusual?"

"Possibly," Kasie hesitantly admitted.

"Well that is ok, the first thing I want you to know is that is perfectly normal. Absolutely expected actually, given what you have been through. Would you like me to refer you to someone to talk to about it further? A female psychologist perhaps?"

Kasie didn't need to consider the suggestion for long, "Yes, thanks Doctor. That would be very helpful."

Kasie felt relieved that what she had recognised was considered normal in a professional's opinion. The doctor had given her a name for a female psychologist who dealt with trauma. He said the psychologist had been working with residents of the town since the tsunami and had built a strong reputation for being quite a specialist in the area.

Returning back to her office, Kasie was enjoying the routine that her work provided. She imagined that each day would get better and she would find her rhythm again. She wondered how much longer she could keep Dee in the country under the pretense that she needed her around now that she had committed to her return to work.

She knew Dee had to get back to her own life, but she wasn't quite ready to say goodbye. Her friend had been overjoyed to get the invite to the mansion party on Saturday night. Having already heard about it from Marco, Dee seemed enthused to also hear that Kasie was keen to go.

Kasie recalled the memory of Dee as she squealed with joy at the news that both of them would be going to the party. As Dee set out to shop for a new party outfit, Kasie had warned her not to spend too much on a dress. As the weather was still warm, that meant a pool party with bikinis and not much else.

Kasie remembered back at the last mansion party dancing with Marco and wondered what it would be like now that he and Dee were becoming friendlier. She wondered if Marco would still find time for a dance and a cocktail with her.

As she returned home that night to her little house, she had barely entered the room before Dee pounced on her. Holding out in her hand for her friend to take to inspect was the tiniest bikini Kasie had ever seen in her life.

"Seriously Dee, where is the rest of it?"

"That's it, why, do you think it is too much?" Dee sounded disappointed.

"Not at all, it is stunning, absolutely gorgeous, it just doesn't leave much to the imagination."

"I have seen smaller on the girls down there at the beach," Dee defended herself.

"Yeah but I think that is more about tan lines. You are going to a pool party at the mansion. I don't think tan lines are your issue." Kasie felt confident enough with her best friend to continue, "I think the fear of seeing Marco with the other women is your issue."

"Ha!" Dee scoffed, "I think you are thinking about your jealous little Prince Charming and his inability to share you with others. Marco and I are just mates. That's it." Dee tried to sound convincing but Kasie wasn't about to believe a word of it.

Kasie smiled, knowing she had hit on a bit of a nerve with Dee. She wondered if Dee really was unaware of how she was feeling towards Marco or just too scared to admit it. Kasie's mind wandered to what her party attire would be for the night. Thinking back to her red bikini, tight white jeans and little red linen shirt from the previous party, she wondered if she should venture out in a dress this time around. She turned to Dee. "Hey do you want to hit the shops again? I need a dress to wear."

"Woohoo!" Dee yelled. "Something super sexy for that gorgeous man of yours."

A thought popped into her head. She did a silent count of the number of people who actually knew anything about her and the party host. It was just a handful of trusted staff, security, Marco and Dee, and of course Tiffany who knew any details of their potential promise to each other.

Her mind skipped ahead to a vision of the party, planned for the following night. Then her mind flipped back again to the memory of the women grabbing their lover and dragging him out of the embrace he shared with Kasie.

She remembered her discomfort at the last party as women all night were attempting to kiss him, jump on his shoulders in the pool or find some excuse to try to sit on his lap. The host being ever so polite, not pushing them away, not attempting to lead them on either she remembered, but certainly not drawing any boundaries around his personal space.

As far as most of the women from The List were concerned, their single bachelor was still hot property. Sure, they may have heard rumours of a fling or a night spent with Kasie, but until he was officially taken off the market, every woman at the upcoming party would be throwing themselves at him in the effort to get his attention.

Maybe he was right about making some sort of announcement, she thought. But the idea of making this still fantasy a reality in any way made her dizzy with anxiety.

"Let's shop!" Kasie snapped herself out of her thoughts, "I need to find the sexiest, slinkiest dress in Coral Cove."

"Yeah, let's go girlfriend." Was Dee's joyful encouragement. She didn't need to be asked twice to spend some quality girlie time with her best friend.

TWELVE

THE PARTY

Saturday afternoon had arrived and the girls were excitedly preparing for the mansion party. Dee walked into Kasie's room holding her hand over the microphone of her phone, "It's him again," she whispered and motioned to her mobile.

Kasie looked up from the precision task of painting her nails and shook her head indicating that she wasn't about to take the call.

"Um sorry, but she is in the shower," Dee lied to the caller, "Ok, see you soon. Can't wait. Bye."

She hung up the call and stood before Kasie, two arms on her hips. Her foot tapping the floor to make it clear to her friend that she wasn't happy, "I don't like lying to him."

"It is not lying, it's just that I am about to hop in the shower, so I didn't have time to talk now anyway."

"What about the other ten times he has called you today?" Dee wasn't about to let her off the hook easily.

"Well, I was busy then too," Kasie lied.

"Why are you avoiding him? You are going to see him in an hour of two anyway, so why don't you just see what he wants to talk to you about. It must be important."

Just then Kasie's message alert sounded again.

"You better respond to that Kasie," she instructed her friend. "Either you do or I will."

Kasie opened the text message:

> *Kase, sorry I keep missing you.*
> *Thought we needed to talk before tonight.*
> *I wondered if you were ready to make an announcement? Xx*

Kasie had no choice but to reply. She couldn't ignore his valid question:

> *Sorry, I am not ready for an announcement yet.*
> *Are you still happy for me to come? Xx*

His reply back was instant:

> *Wouldn't be a party without you.*
> *Are you bringing a toothbrush? Xx*

Dee was now sitting next to Kasie on the bed, "See, not that hard. A couple of text messages would have avoided the constant barrage of phone calls all day. Plus, I still have to get ready. I don't have time to be your full-time personal assistant."

"Well, stop complaining and get ready already. We have a party to get to," Kasie ordered her friend.

Having spent the next two hours, showering, straightening and then curling, painting their nails and applying several layers of lip gloss, the girls were finally ready. As they walked through the door of the mansion, it would be fair to say they both felt confident that they were looking their sexy best, just as they were aiming for.

They graciously accepted the offer of a driver to pick them up from their house and deliver them directly to the mansion's massive front doors.

Marco, the unofficial party greeter was in the grand entry for their arrival, "Holy fuck!" he said as he walked toward the two women. "You two look absolutely amazing. Fuck!" he repeated, "Sexy!"

He looked at Kasie in her micro mini black dress, cut away just enough around the cleavage to suggest a glimpse but nothing more. Her dress finished off with tiny silver beadings around the neckline to add a sparkle to her perfectly made up face.

He glanced toward Dee, wearing shorts that looked like they would have to be cut away to be removed. A low-cut shirt revealing a tiny bikini top and the hint of her perfect breasts.

He hugged them both at the same time, one strong arm around each friend, "I don't know if it is wise to let you inside, maybe I should just take you both up to my room for safe keeping," he laughed as his huge smile lit up his face.

He released the girls from his embrace and looked straight at Dee. His eyes scanned her body from head to toe and back again, "Fuck me babe! You are gorgeous." His brain seemed to be stuck on some strange loop, unable to articulate much more than the basic thought that kept circling through his head.

"If you're lucky," Dee giggled back at him, leaning over to kiss him quickly on the lips.

"Oh, please stop already!" Kasie raised her voice to ensure her message was heard loud and clear, "And I am warning you, if you two leave me alone tonight, I will never speak to either of you again."

The three friends turned toward the noise of the party, "Ladies?" Marco held out his two elbows, outstretched to offer his escort to the two friends, "Let's go make some people insanely jealous."

The party was in full swing, Dee and Kasie timing it to arrive late for maximum impact. Knowing normally Tiffany stole that privilege, tonight they were confident that they had wasted enough time to be the last ones to arrive. Kasie and Dee, led by Marco entered the noisy laughter and loud music of the pool party.

Searching the faces in the crowd, she nervously scanned the room for her very own lover. They passed a waiter, his tray laden with long, cool drinks. Marco released the girls and grabbed a drink for each of them and then finally one for himself.

"Cheers!" he offered as he raised his glass, "Here's to the two most sexy women in the room."

"Cheers!" Both women joined in, sipping their delicious refreshment.

Kasie continued to scan the room. Marco catching a glimpse of what she was searching for helped her out, "He's over there." He pointed toward the bar, "And he's been a good boy all night. I think he has been hanging out for you to arrive." He paused before adding, "God help you when he sees you in that dress though. I don't think even I will be able to save you from his all-consuming advances tonight… or do you not want to be saved tonight?" he added.

"I'm not staying tonight if that is what you are asking me. We have decided to take it slow," Kasie explained.

Marco looked confused and slightly suspicious, "And yet you turn up late and wearing that dress? I don't know if you are trying to fool yourself, but you are definitely not fooling me," Marco challenged her. "And explaining that to him tonight probably won't get you far either."

Their playful conversation was rudely interrupted by Dee, "Oh my god! Look at her!"

All eyes turned back in the direction of the bar. A random wolf whistle escaped the crowd and then another and another. Every eye was now on the gorgeous blonde bombshell standing posing for photos at the edge of the pool beside the bar area. Kasie looked back toward her lover, having stopped mid conversation with the group of guys around him, he too, stood mesmerised by the blonde beauty that was demanding his attention. Several guys took the photo opportunity posing with the woman.

"What the hell is Tiffany wearing?" Dee demanded of her friends.

Marco, barely able to take his eyes off her long enough for his brain to form a response answered with only, "Barely little!"

"What is she doing?" Dee demanded a response again.

Marco having gained some self-control in the last micro second, answered with, "Doing what Tiffany does best. Enjoying being the most watched woman in the room."

The three friends stood still as did every other guest as they continued to watch the side show that was Tiffany. Having wasted enough time with the lowly guests, Tiffany knowing exactly where her target was, began to make her way toward her attentive host.

He stood and watched her walk slowly and surely toward him. Tiffany balanced with perfection on her ten-inch heels, carrying nothing in her hand but her mobile phone and wearing nothing at all beside a flesh coloured monokini. Her attire consisted of a barely there top with a strip of light material flecked with clear crystals covering her large, perfectly enhanced breasts.

The bottom of the swimwear a small triangle held together with a thin string of crystals that formed a long line up her toned stomach to the top. Another string of crystals ran over her hips to the thin piece of flesh coloured material attempting to cover her ample but firm bottom.

Kasie's heart raced as she watched the perfect specimen of a woman close in on their host. As if unable to move, held in place by a trance, he stood still, waiting for her arrival. As she stood before him, she reached out to remove the beer bottle from his hand, passing it without a sound to his friend at his side.

She wasted no time in securing his head between her hands and bringing his lips down to meet hers. The crowd roared with encouragement. Kasie watched horrified as she saw his hands balance gently on her hips as he gave in easily to the kiss. Feeling confident she had secured her prey, Tiffany released his head and ran her hands down his back, stopping eventually on the hard cheeks of his gorgeous bottom.

"What the fuck! Does she want another slap?" Dee yelled above the noise of the crowd as she lunged forward toward the offending couple. Marco was able to grab her arm just in time to stop her from storming across the room and crashing the unfolding scene.

"Don't!" he pleaded with her, "It is just Tiffany being Tiffany. It means nothing."

"It doesn't mean nothing to her," Dee corrected him, motioning towards her best friend, Kasie standing next to them unable to look away.

Sensing she was being watched, Kasie glanced toward the two sets of eyes, looking at her with an overwhelming sense of hurt and shame.

"It's ok," Kasie assured them, "It means nothing." She took a long sip of her drink and watched as Tiffany eventually released her prey and turned to walk away.

Still seemingly stuck in place, their host's eyes followed her as she walked through the crowd and toward the pool. The crowd now more spurred on than ever, let out a thunderous cheer.

Seemingly pleased with her performance and knowing every set of eyes were still on her, Tiffany gracefully slid into the pool and toward the nearest group of her lovely acquaintances. The pool quickly filled with single young men, obviously keen to see if her swimwear became any more translucent when wet.

As the crowd cleared before them, Kasie continued to watch as her host was handed back his beer and he turned his attention back towards his playful group of mates, some clearly chuffed for him, now patting him on the back with sounds of congratulations.

Dee grabbed Kasie in a hug, "Don't worry, he's not into her. She has nothing on you Kasie."

"I'm not worried," Kasie repeated for the benefit of her friends, "But two can play at that game." With that Kasie headed though the crowd and into the direction of the dancefloor.

Marco and Dee looked helplessly at each other. They had been witnesses to this game playing for days now and didn't know how much more of it they could handle. The temperature of the relationship between their two friends ran from freezing cold to blistering hot and all within the space of a few minutes.

"This could be a very long night," Dee uttered with contemplation and dread.

"Well, let's agree that we are not getting involved and get another drink."

"Cheers!" Dee agreed, clinking her glass with Marco's.

It didn't take long for Kasie to get noticed walking through the crowd, "Kasie, Kasie!" She heard the familiar Australian accent call to her in the crowd. She turned around to see a gorgeous mop of streaked blonde hair on an unfamiliar face.

"Kasie!" The thirty-something year old man yelled at her again. She stopped to watch him catch up with her, reaching out to offer his hand, "Kasie isn't it?"

"Yes?" she replied, feeling somewhat unsure.

"Someone told me it was you. I'm Dean."

Kasie felt a faint recognition but not enough to piece together how this gorgeous Australian may know her, "Have we met? I'm sorry. I don't think I remember."

"No, but we have spoken on the phone, Dean... Dean Curtis."

Remembering the name, Kasie was now trying to figure out the link.

The attractive Australian helped her out, "Doctor Dean Curtis from Queensland University. We spoke on the phone, about my research with the Great White Sharks."

The pieces of the puzzle finally fell together, "Oh Dean, I am so sorry. I have had a lot going on lately. I'm sorry I didn't recognise you."
"That's ok. I heard a bit about has happened lately. I am really sorry you had to go through that."

"Thank you," she accepted her colleague's sympathy politely. "You're here in Coral Cove?" Kasie questioned him.

"Yeah, I had some time off and I made a last-minute decision to hop on a plane and come and see the Reef. I hope that is ok!"

"Yes, it's great. I am so pleased to meet you finally."

"Glad to hear." His tone softened as he spoke, "I have been hearing amazing things back home about this sexy Aussie chick doing great things with the reef and I had to come check it out for myself. His eyes glanced down at her short black dress and then back to her face, "And I must say, I am damn glad that I did. Can I get you a drink?" He flicked back his thick, lush blonde hair to peer at her with bright blue eyes, the colour of the ocean surrounding the reef.

"Sure," she smiled back as she allowed him to take her hand in his and lead her to the bar.

Having glanced back to see the brief introduction, Dee now watched as the new couple made their way toward her and Marco standing at the bar. She scanned the room and saw to her horror, their host now also watching Kasie as he marched toward the two of them. Dee tugged on Marco's pants as he ordered a drink for both of them, "Marco, you had better watch this."

Kasie reached the bar first and immediately began with her introduction of her new friend.

"As yes," Marco smiled, "We met earlier. How are you enjoying your night so far Dean?"

"Well it has been very entertaining and looks to be only getting better," he responded as his eyes ran up and down the length of Kasie's tanned, toned legs.

"Well that's good to hear Dean." The strong and slightly irritated voice of their host responded. He had appeared seemingly out of nowhere to join his friends at the bar.

Kasie looked up to witness her lover standing beside her. "Good evening beautiful," he added without delay. "You are late," he said, bending down to kiss her on the lips.

Dean looked from Kasie toward their host and back again, obviously trying to make clearer in his head the relationship between the two.

Their host continued, "Kasie, do you have a moment? I would like to talk to you."

"Actually," Kasie replied in defiance, "Dean and I were just getting a drink and getting acquainted. I wasn't aware he was coming, but you seemed to know, given that Dean received an invite to your party. A phone call would have been nice."

"Actually Kase, I have been trying to phone you all day," her host replied back, the irritation rising in his tone.

Kasie sensed his frustration but feeling equally upset with the scene that she just witnessed, wasn't about to give in, "How about you spread yourself around to your other equally valuable guests and you and I can talk later."

He was furious with her act of defiance, but rather than let it play out in front of his guests, he turned and departed as instructed.

"He's your boss, isn't he?" Dean checked for clarification the moment the host was out of earshot.

"Yes, unfortunately at times, but yes he is my boss," Kasie replied.

"And was that nearly naked blonde his girlfriend or wife?" Dean enquired.

"Neither!" Dee was quick to respond.

"Well it's kind of complicated," Kasie offered by way of explanation.

"That's ok, she wasn't my type anyway. A bit too overdramatic for my liking," he continued. "I prefer a woman who is sexy without having to try to be. A bit like you," he flirted with Kasie.

Marco shook his head, "You Aussies sure do say it how it is. Don't you?"

"Yep," Dee agreed as she raised her glass. "Cheers to us Aussies taking over Coral Cove for the night."

"Cheers!" The fun-loving foursome toasted with their drinks in unison.

Their host watched on from afar as the four new friends took a swig of their drinks. He was furious that Kasie was behaving like she was and concerned also that her actions may have meant that she had already experienced a change of heart regarding their relationship.

THIRTEEN

THE NEW FRIEND

Several cocktails later and Kasie and Dean were tearing up the dancefloor. They weren't surprised to find that they were similar in so many ways. They roared with laughter and jumped with joy when the DJ played a familiar song from one of their favourite Australian bands. The two Aussies yelled over the music in unison. As the song ended, Kasie suggested another drink. Dancing was after all, very thirsty work.

As Dean ordered their drinks, Kasie realised that she was suddenly feeling a little homesick. She had enjoyed the last few hours in the company of a fellow Australian, especially one that was so good looking. She had an idea that she would take a selfie to post online for her friends back home… the caption to read; *Two crazy Aussies catching up in this South Pacific Island Paradise.* She searched for her phone.

"Ah," she mouthed the sound as she realised that she had given her phone to Dee to keep safe in her bag while she danced. She looked around the room for any sign of Dee or Marco. The crowd was mostly in the pool or on the dancefloor as was normal by this stage of the night. She scanned the room again to find one very serious and sexy set of eyes looking back at her.

She held his glance for a moment. He smiled a huge grin and mouthed the words, "I love you," to her.

She smiled back at her lover and said silently to him, "I love you too." The fun of the night had allowed her to feel a little less jealous about the whole Tiffany kissing scene and she realised she had probably been a bit harsh with her potential future husband.

"I have to find my phone," she explained to Dean as she moved from the bar.

"But I just got us drinks," Dean pleaded.

"I will be right back. I just need to find Dee. Don't start without me," she laughed as she made her way into the crowd.

Having searched the pool area, kitchen and downstairs entertaining area, Kasie feared there was only one place they could be. She made her way upstairs in search for the wayward lovers. She followed the long luxuriously appointed hallways to the room that Dee had stayed in. Knocking on the large wooden frame, she yelled her name, "Dee, Marco, are you decent?"

There was silence. She turned the handle gently and opened the door, seeing clearly through the light of the moon and the party lights searing through the window, she could tell the room was unoccupied. Closing the door again, she made her way to the room she began to think of for a short time, as her own.

Knocking again, she yelled through the door, "Marco, Dee. Are you in there?"

Opening the large, heavy door, she again found a room with no inhabitants. Thinking that she should use this time to visit the bathroom she walked inside and closed the door behind her. Knowing the room well enough, she brushed past the bed and into the adjoining bathroom without needing the assistance of the bedroom light. She glanced at her face in the mirror and wished she had some lip-gloss for a quick touch up. She remembered that too was in Dee's bag. She wondered where she could be.

Deep in her own thoughts as she stepped from the bathroom and into the barely lit room, she didn't see him until she ran straight into his hard, strong chest. His hands were immediately on her, his lips immediately began pressing down on her mouth. Without seeing his face, she recognised his smell, his strong hands on her and the taste of his sweet mouth. She wrapped her arms around him as their mouths moved together. Her body immediately began to respond to his touch.

This unconscious control he had over her entire length of her body was indescribable. Her hands were finding his chest and slowly she began unbuttoning his clean, crisp shirt. He stopped her after the first button, and placed his hands on hers and peeled them from his shirt.

He held her hands in front of her clasped together and looked into her eyes. His evil smile now lit up the dim room, "Do you remember what I said I would do to you, if you ever made me jealous again?"

She swallowed hard as she remembered his words, her body tensing with anticipation. Her nipples becoming erect and her panties moist from the mere thought of what this man was about to do to her.

"No," she lied back to him.

"I said that if you ever made me jealous again, I would pull down your panties and smack your bare bottom with this hand." He raised his right palm as if to display the intoxicating weapon.

She released her hands from his and smiled widely as she slowly turned around and lifted her dress to reveal her small black G-string.

He tried to grab her but she was too fast. She made her way toward the bathroom. He began his chase. She stopped and swerved at the very last minute to hide behind the large lounge in the middle of the room. He stood the other side of the lounge, arms at his side, eagerly planning his next move.

She giggled sexily as he lunged over the lounge in a vain attempt to reach her. She laughed and positioned herself behind a second chair. She noticed the moonlight seeping through the sheer curtain and purposely stood directly into the light.

He watched her eyes as she stared intently at him. She dropped her hands down to the hem of the dress, and maintained her stare on him. She smiled as she lifted the dress over her underwear, past her stomach, to reveal her naked breasts. She finally lifted the dress over her head and giggled as she threw the tiny dress directly into his face.

"That's a shame," he smiled at her. "You looked fucking hot in that dress."

"And now?" she flirted with him.

"Now?" he paused. "You look totally fuckable!"

He ran around the chair once again failing to catch her. She ran toward the bed and jumped straight onto it. She stood still, legs apart, her chest heaving in and out at the excitement of the chase and the impending foreplay. He stood at the end of the bed taking in the sight of the woman he loved.

He slowly unbuttoned his shirt, then his pants, dropping them both on the ground. He crawled onto the bed, reaching towards her to grab her ankle with enough force to drop her straight onto the huge, soft mattress. He crawled up the length of her body, placing his weight on top of her as he kissed her mouth once again. His large hand found her breast and began tantalising it with his fingers.

Her hands were roaming his entire body as if not sure what part of the hard surface she wanted to feel next. His body moved with hers and they found the perfect fit.

"Oh, fuck Kase, you're so sexy," he hissed the words through his passionate groans. "I have to feel you," he moaned.

She placed her hand on his chest as if to hit the pause button. She pushed gently to create a small gap between their two hot bodies. She smiled at him as she pushed him away. She took in every inch of his chest, his toned stomach and his small, white underwear. She took her time to speak, feeling his breath in and out. His desire for her was beyond control.

She bit her lip, and smiled again at the thought of what she was about to do to him. "You look like you need something to take the edge off," she mimicked his words from just days earlier.

He smiled back at her, understanding immediately the implication of her suggestion. She used both hands to push his chest further away until his back was flat on the bed. She licked her lips as she made her way down the bed to his underwear. He didn't stop her but instead lay still, anxious for her touch. She removed his underwear to reveal her man very much ready for what he was about to receive.

She licked her lips again as her eyes met his for the final time before she moved her head to his toned abs, kissing them gently, letting her lips and tongue linger on the hot skin as she slowly moved her mouth down to his penis. She couldn't see his face, but imagined his smile as she began to exert her control over him.

After a short time and feeling very pleased with herself for her strong self-control, Kasie headed down the stairs just a step ahead of the host. Feeling like two guilty teenagers, they looked ahead to see who might be wandering the house ready to catch them. He stopped her on the steps.

"Did you bring your toothbrush?" he smiled at her.

"No, but now I wish I did," she joked back at him.

"But you are staying, aren't you?" he pleaded with her.

"No, not tonight. There is plenty of time for that. No rush… remember?" she emphasised the last three words.

"Kase, you are killing me. I sincerely need to be with you." And she knew that meant not just in the literal sense of the word.

"I think you were right about not rushing things," she finally let him know.

He paused for a moment understanding the meaning behind her words, "Ok," he relented.

"I love you," he added one final time.
"I love you too," she smiled at him and planted a sneaky kiss on his lips.

As the two lovers re-entered the party location they went their separate ways, not yet ready to share their joyous news of their relationship with the world. Kasie spotted Dee straight away, giving Tiffany a run for her money in the arena of tiny bathing suits. She watched Dee lap up the attention of the hunky thirty-something men surrounding her.

Having finally located Dee's discarded bag in the kitchen, Kasie had changed quickly into her own bikini ready for a refreshing dip after her physical exertions. Kasie walked over to the sunbed and lifted her glittering black dress over her head to reveal her new, tiny black G-string bikini. She could feel the eyes on her.

She walked toward Dee in the shallow end of the pool and stepped down onto the top ledge of the clear blue water. She paused and looked up at the gorgeous man standing in front of her at the edge of the pool. Her lover's face awash with pure anguish as if she was stepping into a flooded river filled with man-eating crocodiles.

She smiled at him and stared into his eyes as he watched her step slowly into the cool, refreshing liquid. She smiled as one of his companions punched him in the arm as he tried to break his trance-like stare to gain his attention. His friend tilted his head toward her as if encouraging his host to connect with his now nearly naked guest.

Kasie took the last step into the cool water, touching the bottom of the pool with her feet. As she did, she felt a pair of strong, masculine arms at her hips. As if in reflex, she paused and looked up to her lover. His hand tightening around his glass, his fury obvious as his face reddened with anger.

She heard the again familiar accent as Dean put his face near hers and asked her, "Where have you been? I've been waiting for you?"

Kasie continued to make her way toward Dee, who was now looking back at her with great concern. She tried to ignore the strong hand, which had found its place at the small of her back. She dared not look back to her lover.

Dee was quick to save her from her new admirer and rushed through the water toward Kasie. Dee threw her arms around her. She placed a protective arm around her shoulder to push her toward the in-pool seating and positioned herself to stand protectively between Kasie and Dean. Dee turned to Dean, "Hey do you want to grab us some drinks mate?" she asked with her best exaggerated Australian accent.

"Sure!" he replied. "What will it be?"

"Surprise us," Dee replied with enthusiasm to distract their new friend for a few minutes.

Dean looked at Kasie and smiled, "Be right back, don't go anywhere."

Dee immediately began her interrogation, "What the hell are you doing Kasie?"

"Nothing, I wasn't doing anything, we were just dancing and drinking and talking about Queensland. I guess I was a little homesick and I got caught up hearing his stories from back home."

"Yes, so that explains that, what about you and lover boy over there? Where were the two of you? Don't you think that I noticed the two of you missing for ages?"

"Well, I was looking for you and Marco, if you must know. I couldn't find you anywhere."

"Well, I haven't left the party, except for a quick check of the make-up of course. Marco on the other hand, has been busy with his other friends." Dee glanced towards the dancefloor and the very relaxed Marco dancing with the near naked Tiffany. "I thought he had more taste than that," she spat out the last few words.

"That woman!" she added in despair. "What is the spell she holds over these men?"

"Dee, if you hadn't noticed, you weren't doing too badly yourself before I rudely distracted you from your audience of hopeful and very horny men."

Kasie paused, a question coming to mind, "Do you think it is wrong for a woman to use her um… womanly charms to attract or tease a man?" Kasie continued.

"If I thought it was wrong for just a minute, do you think I would have bought this bikini?" Dee laughed. "Speaking of which, where the hell were you hiding that tiny piece of an excuse for swimwear you are wearing?"

Kasie laughed, "I don't know actually, these things just keep turning up in my bags. A present from our kind host, I suspect."

"Oh, is that why he is trying to pierce your heart with his x-ray vision eyes right now?"

Kasie didn't dare glance up at her lover who was obviously unhappy with the attention Kasie was receiving tonight from not only her new Australian friend but the bevy of hunky men now forming around her and Dee.

Dee offered a final word of advice on the subject, "Kasie, I think it is perfectly fine for a woman to use every tool that Mother Nature gave her. It just isn't an equal playing field if we don't."

"Mmm." Kasie's mind was catapulted to moments earlier when her tool had been her mouth, performing skillfully and masterfully, having full control of her gorgeous lover. "And I guess, it isn't as if they complain about it, at least not most of the time," Kasie added.

Dee responded, "The only time they complain about our womanly charms is when they are not the complete and sole receiver of their little pleasures."

"Enough already," Dee demanded, our hunky little Aussie mate is due to return with our drinks and there is fun to be had in the mansion tonight. I have waited long enough for a party here, so I am going to enjoy myself. Marco is!" she glanced back again to the dancefloor and Marco, now hands all over Tiffany's seemingly naked torso.

On cue, their new friend returned with cocktails for everyone. "One more toast to kick start the night," Dee yelled. "To my Aussie mates!"

Her two friends completed the toast, "To mates!" The three friends laughed and sculled their drinks.

Dean was first to finish his beverage and place his glass precariously on the edge of the pool. He watched as his two friends finished the last of the clear liquid in their shot glasses and placed them too beside his.

Taking a breath, Dean slipped quietly under the surface, seeing clearly the women's outlines in the clear water. He reached forward and grabbed both of them, one pair of legs in each of his strong arms. He raised his body and head above the surface of the water, strategically placing both women, one on each shoulder.

Submerging himself again in the cool water, he took both women with him. Performing a version of a crocodile death roll, he spun the women around under the water before releasing them to again take a breath.

As they emerged from the depths of the water, the three friends laughed raucously. Happy to be having fun, the girls couldn't have cared less about the damage to their makeup or their perfectly straightened hair. Oblivious to the familiar onlookers, the girls made a silent pact to team up against their strong new friend as they began their retaliated attack.

They both jumped on Dean and pushed him under the surface of the water again. Not daring to glance in the direction of their host, the girls enjoyed the laughter and innocent fun of their new game.

Marco had now joined his boss at the side of the pool, and stared toward the two women laughing playfully with their new

Australian friend. He reached out and took the glass from his friend's hand, "Sorry boss, but you are a second away from impaling that glass into your hand. If you are trying to not look madly in love with that girl in the tiny black bikini, you are not doing a very good job. You couldn't be any more obvious if you tried."

His boss stared intently remaining silent as he watched the three of them playfully laughing in the pool. He watched as Dean once again reached for Kasie, grabbing her slender waist in his hands as he pulled her down on top of him under the water.

He couldn't tear his eyes away from the threesome playing in the pool. Every time Dean's hands touched Kasie his breath caught in his throat. He felt the heat rise in his face. His muscles ached from tensing. His mouth had become dry as he struggled to tear himself away from the scene in front of him.

He wasn't normally a jealous man and certainly never a violent one. But right now, all he could think of was grabbing his Kasie and taking her away from everything, so that no one could ever touch her again.

He heard Marco beside him but hadn't acknowledged his words. He knew he was correct. He wasn't doing a good job at fooling anyone about his intentions for this woman. He was trying to take it slowly at her request. All he had wanted to do was to make the announcement, make it tonight. Tell the world that he planned on marrying this very woman, his Kasie and making her, his own. But at Kasie's insistence he had remained silent and not let anyone know that The List and his plans to date were now a distant memory.

Dean lunged toward Kasie again, appearing all too familiar for the host's liking. He grabbed her waist and dragged her under the water. Who was this foreign stranger and why had he suddenly appeared out of nowhere to create this disturbance in his life? He planned to get some more information on this conservationist in the morning. He didn't know what his intentions were being here but planned to make it perfectly apparent to him that he wasn't welcome here. And he certainly wasn't welcome to place his filthy little hands on his Kase.

"Ok, boss, you are scaring me now. I don't want to be the one left communicating with the police interrogation over a dead visiting Australian marine researcher… even though he is an annoying player," Marco added.

His boss remained still and silent.

"Ok, sorry boss, but I have to do this." He reached over and grabbed his boss, without delay he dragged him to the edge of the pool and threw him into the water. There as always to provide the added support and security, Marco dived into the clear water immediately behind him.

The two men swam to the shallow end of the pool, reaching the trio of Australians as they emerged once again to catch their breath. Sensing the tension, the women stopped still in their tracks. Their friend oblivious to the danger behind him was laughing as he tried to regain his breath through his laughter.

Marco and his boss, now both removing their shirts on their approach, were nearing their destination. Moving, one to either side of the young Australian, the men stood still. Both girls watched nervously in anticipation, waiting for who would make the next move.

Their host was the first to speak, "Looks like these girls are giving you some trouble, do you need a hand mate?" he asked of Dean, mimicking his best Aussie accent, honed to perfection of course by his time spent with Kasie.

"Ha, nah, thanks but I think I can handle them," was Dean's arrogant response to his two new and unwelcome male companions.

Unaccustomed to waiting for approval or permission, their host took what he came for. Reaching forward he grabbed at Kasie's waist, pulling her into the deep end of the large pool. "I'll take this one off your hands," he playfully yelled back to Dean.

Kasie snuggled into her captor's arms, and wrapped her long legs around his body. She swung her slender arms around his neck for support. She pushed her exposed cleavage into his chest as she began to kiss his lips. He kissed her back and forgetting for a moment where they were, he pinned her body against the side of the pool, firmly holding her in place with the force of his strong, hard torso. He closed his eyes and kissed the woman that he loved.

Completely forgetting his surroundings, he cupped his hands under her naked cheeks, pushing her towards him and onto his hardness. The crowd roared with encouragement yet again. The sounds of the crowd didn't quite break through the passion of the moment for the two lovers until a nearby supporter yelled loudly next to them.

Kasie and her host sheepishly looked around at the now forming crowd. She glanced back at Dee, Dean and Marco still paddling in the shallow water. She couldn't help but notice Tiffany now standing at the side of the pool, her mouth open with shock at the scene she just witnessed.

Kasie released herself from his embrace, playfully splashing water into his face she joked with him for the benefit of their cover, "Hands off you leech!"

Her host smiled at her as he realised instantly that Kasie was trying to distract attention away from them. He addressed his audience, "Hey I tried," he laughed as he shrugged his shoulders.

Kasie made her way back to her friends. Dean still shell-shocked by the audacity of Kasie's boss, turned to Dee and asked, "What will his little blonde girlfriend have to say about that?"

"It's kind of complicated," Marco smirked as he replied.

FOURTEEN

THE CONTENDER

The now wet host leapt onto the side of the pool and walked with genuine purpose toward the small pool house behind the bar. He reached into the tall white shelving and grabbed himself a towel. He held his towel over his face for a moment and sighed a huge sigh into the soft material.

"What the hell was that?" the voice beside him screamed at him.

He lowered his towel to reveal Tiffany standing at his side, translucent monokini still miraculously held in place by the lines of sparkling white crystals.

He felt confused by her obvious anger toward him, "What do you mean?"

"That, that kiss, what was that all about?" she demanded to know.

He sighed again, feeling too exhausted to be having this conversation right now. "I still don't understand what you are asking me? What is wrong? Why are you so upset?"

"Why, am I upset? Because you made me look like a fool."

"Tiff, what are you talking about?" he begged her for an explanation.

"After our kiss before, to then go and do that to her. It is just disrespectful. How do you think it makes me look?"

"Tiff, I didn't kiss you remember. You kissed me."

This just angered Tiffany more. "Exactly, and just then you practically assaulted Kasie. You have never kissed me like that. You made it look like…" she stopped, not wanting to say what she feared she saw behind the kiss.

"I am sorry Tiff, I didn't mean to hurt you, but you of all people. I thought you understood…" his voice trailed off.

"Understood what?" she demanded of him. "I understand that you care for Kasie. I know that I saw you kiss her that night she was here alone in the mansion with you. I know you were worried about her, when she disappeared, as we all were. I also understand, that she has now returned to work and you are her employer. Do you really think this is appropriate behavior between an employer and employee?"

The realisation hit him that Tiffany didn't understand as much as he had given her credit for. Remembering back to the day she came to the mansion to show her concern for him after Kasie's disappearance, he imagined then that Tiffany had realised the depth of his feelings for the Australian woman. He sighed again as he realised Tiffany didn't actually know at all what had been transpiring between the two of them. He let out another huge sigh.

He knew Kasie wasn't ready to tell the world yet about their plans for a future together. He needed to respect Kasie's wishes but in doing so he was forced to lie to Tiffany about the extent of his feelings for the visiting Aussie.

"I am so sorry Tiff. It was just a bit of fun. I didn't mean to upset you. I meant no disrespect for anyone," he apologised with genuine sincerity.

Tiffany's face softened with the apology. She took her cue to walk toward him and wrap her small arms around his hard, naked wet torso. "Maybe I could believe that apology more if we kissed and made up," she glanced up at him with a hopeful, whimsical smile as he leant down and kissed her lips.

She responded with enthusiasm, running her hands over his strong body, finding his hands and placing them on hers. The kiss didn't last long, but it was long enough for one very confused party guest to catch it from beginning to end.

* * *

Having watched her friend jump from the pool, Kasie also climbed out of the pool and decided to follow him as he made his way to the nearby pool house. Wanting to check on him, Kasie thought she could catch a couple of minutes alone with him to find out if there was anything they needed to do after their short lapse of caution in the pool. Kasie stopped short of walking into the pool house, having caught the tail end of a very private conversation.

She couldn't believe her ears as she heard her lover say to the pretty, young guest in his company. "I am so sorry Tiff, it was just a bit of fun. I didn't mean to upset you."

Kasie watched as he apologised with genuine sincerity. Her shock was compounded as she watched her lover bend down and kiss the woman on the mouth.

Unsure of what she was seeing unfold in front of her, Kasie couldn't move. She couldn't speak. She watched as the kiss ended. His face pulled away from Tiffany. Her eyes still closed as she savoured every last second of the moment. She had seen enough. She turned and ran toward the pool.

As she reached over the edge, she grabbed Dee's hand from the side of the pool and got her immediate attention, "We have to go now Dee," she ordered her.

"Kasie, what is it? What's going on? Are you ok?"

"I'll explain everything, I just need to leave now, please, hurry."

Without further explanation, Dee hastily retreated from the pool, leaving a confused pairing of Marco and Dean without explanation as to her sudden departure.

Joining Kasie at the side of the pool, her slinky black dress now in her hand, Dee grabbed her spare hand and started towards the exit. They were stopped mid step as directly in front of them Tiffany and their party host re-appeared from the pool house.

Having just stepped out from the pool house, hand in hand, the beautiful Tiffany and the party host made a strange paring.

Dee opened her mouth to speak as Kasie pulled at her hand to keep her grounded in place. She feared a backlash of anger from Dee directed again toward her least liked person in the room, Tiffany.

From behind the two girls, a male voice spoke just loud enough to be heard above the pounding music. Dee and Kasie turned to see Dean now standing dripping wet beside them.

Turning his full attention to Kasie, once again accentuating his full Australian accent playfully he asked her, "When will I get to see you again Kasie?"

Kasie looked into the playful blue eyes of her new friend. Without speaking she turned around and looked at the intense green stare of her host.

She turned toward Dean and without answering, put her moist lips on his. Having been thinking of nothing but kissing these gorgeous plump lips since the moment he met her, Dean saw this as an act of good fortune. He pulled her gently from Dee's hold and kissed her back.

As she released herself from the embrace after a moment or two, Kasie replied to Dean's question, "Come to the office Monday, we can talk then."

She turned toward the now enraged face of her host and grabbed Dee's hand once more and made their exit.

Still standing frozen, the host turned his full attention to the young blonde man in front of him. Releasing Tiffany's hand, he strode toward him.

"What the hell do you think you are doing?" he demanded of his guest. He was beyond outraged to think of anyone touching his Kasie in that way.

"What do you think?" his rival answered, "You think you own all of these gorgeous women? You have your pretty little thing there, why don't you back off Kasie and show some fucking loyalty mate!"

The dark-haired host, fuming with rage, stepped closer, standing just a few inches above his guest, his bulk, height and frame would have been intimidating to any other contender. "You have no idea what is going on here, so just back the fuck away." His anger at the unwelcome guest was evident.

"I think I have seen enough tonight to know that you, Mr. Rich Boy, think that you own these people. You treat them like your fucking servants and the girls like your personal sex slaves. Kasie doesn't deserve to be treated like that. She is an amazing woman!"

"You think I don't know that?" his host challenged Dean.

"You certainly don't look like you give a fuck, that's for sure. Why don't you just take the little Missus here and leave Kasie the fuck alone." With that the man stepped slightly sideways and gave his host a hard shoulder barge as he moved past him."

His host, never a man who had been challenged so publicly before, turned and grabbed his guest by the arm, halting him dead in his tracks. The two men stopped and stared each other down, each waiting for the other to make the first move.

Marco just catching for the first time the altercation between the two men, rushed toward them. He stepped between them, close enough to be heard as he said in a soft calming tone, "Now gentlemen that will be enough for tonight." He turned his attention to Dean and instructed the new guest. "Probably best if you leave now. There will be a car outside to take you back to your hotel."

The host finally released his grasp on his guest's arm to reveal a bright red mark where his strong hand had hold. The two men finally broke their stare and stepped apart. Dean took his orders and made his way to the front of the mansion and to the waiting car as he grabbed his clothes and a dry towel on the way.

"What the hell was that?" Marco demanded of his boss.

"That arrogant shite. He thinks I disrespected Kasie. He has no fucking idea what he is saying. Who the hell does he think he is?" his boss ranted.

Marco smiled. The tension now gone as his boss was left to vent. "Did he hit a raw nerve there, boss?"

FIFTEEN

THE ISLAND

Kasie woke the next day feeling as if she was in a recurring nightmare. She and her lover get close. She begins to feel the rumblings of true love when a minute later it seems, something or someone steps in and rips it out from under her. She had become exhausted with all the push and pull of their new relationship.

One day he was crazy for her. The next, he was pushing her away or intent on slowing things down. He pursued her relentlessly at the last party she attended at the mansion and this time, it appeared Tiffany was becoming the focus of his obsessions.

"Arrgh!" she yelled out into the empty bedroom. "Men!"

Just at that moment a text message signaled her to start her day:

Good morning gorgeous. Hope you slept well.
Would you like to catch up for coffee today? Dean

She read the message, yelled at the empty room once more. She replaced her phone on the bedside table and pulled the covers up and over her head. She closed her eyes and willed herself to fall back to sleep. She wasn't ready to face the reality of what the day would bring. She was just drifting back into a peaceful slumber when her phone demanded her attention once more.

A message from him:

Kase, we need to talk. Tell me where and when. Xx

"Ha." That about sums it up… two men, two polar opposites. Dean, her new acquaintance was happy, cheerful, carefree and easygoing. So very unlike her intense, jealous and serious boss. Dean was probably the way he was as a result of growing up in the beautiful sunshine state, as Queensland is best known as.

Like her, Dean grew up near the beach, living a pretty carefree lifestyle where the most drama you have is if the waves are flat. Dean lived most of his life on the Gold Coast whereas Kasie lived a couple hours flying time away in the Northern part of Queensland, her small town of Port Douglas being where she spent most of her life.

Kasie realised she had a lot in common with Dean. The two of them, both fit and loving their outdoors lifestyle, which resulted she imagined in their combined love of the ocean and later the pull of the important conservation work they both specialised in. Having followed Dean's research for some time now, she was surprised they hadn't met long before now. Though she imagined, she had really only started to make her mark in the conservation field with her latest project here at Coral Cove.

Her mind turned to her other text message and the demanding, domineering style of her intent and intense boss. Dark, brooding, foreboding, his passion was unmistakable. Having lived a similarly charmed childhood by the ocean, he also enjoyed a love of nature and obviously had a mission to ensure the survival of the local ecology.

But somehow his drive was different, maybe as a result of growing up having this insane sense of responsibility instilled in him from an early age. From the outside, he was a man focused on a mission. The sole heir left to, and without choice, continue his family's important work.

His loyalty to this town and to its people was unwavering. But there was a collective feeling from what she had gathered in her short time here that people felt a sense of comfort, of safety and security knowing that he was their unofficial leader, the representative responsible for their beloved town's financial and ecological future. Their respective loyalty in return to him from everyone in the town was undeniable.

"Arrgh!" she yelled out again to the empty room. "Men!"

Dee opened the door with a morning greeting and a smile, "I'm not sure if you are placing an order for any particular man but you might need to be more specific, are you wanting blonde and fun loving or dark, sexy and controlling?" Dee laughed at herself.

"Neither!" Kasie yelled back at her, picking up her phone and offering it to Dee to read.

Reading both the messages, she smiled to her friend, "Well, you could have more serious issues, like say running out of coffee!" her friend offered.

"Please don't tell me we are out." Kasie's morning was just getting worse by the minute.

"We are after this cup," Dee replied, handing the warm beverage to her grateful friend.

"What should I do, Dee?" Kasie begged her for an answer.

"Do nothing!" This was her simple solution to the problem. "Let's just get a car and head to the beach. Just you and me and our little bikinis. Let's go work on my tan before I have to head home," Dee offered as a suggestion.

"Sounds great," Kasie agreed. Sitting up, feeling more excited than a minute ago, she had a great idea. "I know just the place, but we have to get to the wharf and borrow a boat first."

"Sounds like an adventure, get dressed and let's head out. It is a beautiful day out there," Dee replied.

Kasie sculled the last of the coffee from the cup, turned off her mobile phone, and did the unthinkable. She opened her bedside drawer, placed the phone gently inside and closed the drawer.

Having made it out of the house in record time for fear of unexpected guests arriving at their door, the two women made their way to the wharf, rented a small boat for the day and headed to Long Island.

"It is absolutely gorgeous here!" Dee sighed as the boat carefully skimmed over the reef and neared the white sandy beach.

"Isn't it?" Kasie's words sent a small shiver up her back as the memory of her last visit here echoed in her mind.

As they pulled up to the beach, the two women dragged the boat a short distance up and onto the sand. They stretched as they stood and looked toward the clear blue water. They were silent as they stood in awe of the natural beauty around them.

The ringing of Dee's phone broke through the serenity of the scene. As if by reaction rather than thought, Dee answered the phone. Her face immediately turned to Kasie as she searched for a response. Kasie shook her head to confirm Dee's suspicions.

"Umm, I'm sorry. I just don't think she is ready to talk to you yet. Give her some time hey?" She offered some comfort to the obviously emotional man on the other end of the phone. "Ok, bye," she spoke gently as she ended the call.

"Do you want to know what he said?" Dee asked her friend.

"No," was Kasie's quick and definite reply. She wasn't ready to talk to him and she wasn't ready to hear any more excuses from him about his behaviour the night before. She just wanted to be away from the drama for the day. Jumping into the salt water of the ocean always made everything feel better.

"Let's go swimming," Kasie changed the subject quickly as she grabbed her snorkel gear and fins. With practiced precision, she was fully equipped and in the water, while her friend was still removing her sundress.

Dee watched as Kasie, looking like she belonged to the sea itself, dove into the clear, calm water in front of her.

The two friends enjoyed a relaxing and carefree day on the island, choosing to return only when the sun threatened its retreat as it lowered itself into the horizon. Motoring back at a leisurely pace, Dee thought it pertinent to raise the subject again. "Kasie, what are you going to do now?" she asked her friend with a hint of concern.

"I don't know," Kasie was quick to answer.

"Are you going to speak to him?" Dee continued.

"Not yet. I don't know what I want to say just yet." Kasie's tone was a mixture of confusion and sadness.

"Why don't you just hear him out, let him explain what happened. Maybe there is some logical reason for what you saw," Dee offered by way of explanation.

"It's not just that. It's just that part of me feels that it shouldn't be this hard. Do you know what I mean?" She turned to

Dee, "That is, if we were truly meant to be together, then it wouldn't feel this hard and…" she paused, "and it wouldn't hurt this much."

"No pain, no gain," Dee offered rather lightheartedly.

Kasie looked toward her friend. She realised she was just looking out for her but she also knew she had a soft spot for their friend and would want her to hear him out. Kasie really didn't know if her own inexperience in this area was creating a sense of naivety in her about how much work relationships were. All she really had to judge them by was her own parents and a few of her friends who had already managed to find true love.

From the outside these relationships to her seemed effortless. She knew her father and mother had fought sometimes, of course every couple did, but she had never known her parents to cause this level of emotional hurt or uncertainty in each other.

The same for her friends, she had watched their relationships grow, attended their engagements and weddings and looked on as they appeared to go from strength to strength together. She just wasn't sure if she and her lover had the right combination to make this work.

Everything used to be easy between them. They used to debate, disagree and laugh together as friends. She loved spending time with him. It felt effortless but that had all changed in the last few weeks. After that party and the physical attraction between them grew, everything was different. She wanted nothing more than to go back in time and reconnect with her friend that she now missed so much.

And yesterday, in walked Dean, this carefree, easygoing but incredibly sexual Aussie researcher. Everything about the few hours they shared together was energising, invigorating and fun. She hadn't laughed that much ever. And even with what was nothing more than clearly a friendship based on mutual values and respect for each other's work, she could readily admit, he was one of the most stunning men she had ever met.

Dean was all of this and all in such a humble and unassuming kind of way. She imagined him in his board shorts, surfboard under the arm, making his way down the sand to Snapper Rocks on the Gold Coast. She pictured every set of female eyes on him and him probably not having even a clue as to the attention he was receiving.

Meeting Dean yesterday just accentuated the vast differences of the two men vying for her attention at the party. Like the ocean that surrounded her now in the tiny boat as she sailed back to shore. Dean was the reef, light, open, beautiful, inviting and drawing people to him. On the other hand, her employer, the man who had asked her to marry him, he was the deep dark ocean beyond. Unknown, mysterious, somewhat dangerous and ever changing, offering up small surprises without fully exposing the deep recessed not able to be seen to the naked eye.

"Arrgh Men!" Kasie said out loud once more.

"Yes, you keep saying that Kasie," Dee responded to her, "But surely you have enough on your plate without requesting any more from the universe!"

The women enjoyed a beautiful day on the reef. Dee had heard so much from Kasie in her phone calls home to begin to imagine what the reef was like but not now, not until today, could she fully comprehend its true awesomeness.

Kasie's house was quiet and empty when the girls finally returned home. Thankfully, she thought to herself, she just didn't have the energy tonight to deal with anyone, let alone the intensity of the man who was chasing her down to speak to her all day.

She walked softly into her bedroom, fearing the worst. She sat on the edge of the bed, opened her bedside drawer and turned on her phone. She closed her eyes as she heard the sound of the phone drawing to life. She opened her eyes just in time to see the message indicator, spinning through the numbers, all messages from him. She opened the first message:

Kase, please call me. I need to see you.
I need to know what last night was all about. Xx

And another:

Please Kase, I love you. I am scared I am losing you.
Please message or call me. Xx

And yet another:

Kase, I am trying to leave you alone but I am worried about you.
Worried about what happened last night. Please let me know you are ok. Xx

Kasie felt a slight tinge of guilt at her avoidance of her friend, obviously allowing the events of the night before to ruminate in his head. She held her phone in her hand, contemplating whether or not to respond. She looked skywards as if the answer would come to her. She began to type in her reply:

I'm fine, don't worry. I just need some time.
I will speak to you soon. xx

His reply was instant:

I love you xx

She didn't respond. She didn't know for sure how she was feeling. She could commit to those words, but not to the implication of what else came with them right now. Not with all honesty, she thought to herself.

SIXTEEN

THE OFFICE

Kasie woke early to begin her next work day. Having restocked their coffee supplies the day earlier, she finished the remnants of her cup before heading out the door. One final stop to check her face in the mirror, she paused. Speaking softly to herself as to not wake her sleeping guest in the adjoining room, she looked into her reflection and sighed, "Here we go!"

The research facility car park was still quiet by the time she had arrived. Stepping through the front doors of the huge reception area, she was greeted by the as always smiling, Rachel, "Good morning, Miss McCarthy," Rachel beamed at her. "You have a guest waiting for you."

Kasie followed Rachel's line of sight to see the probable reason for her rather overly pleasant mood this morning.

"Good morning gorgeous," was Dean's warm welcome to Kasie. He walked toward her and smiled as he stepped closer and leaned in to kiss her mouth. Kasie's face flushed from a slight awkwardness at being caught so off guard.

Feeling the need to explain this hunky specimen of a man now standing beside her, Kasie turned again to Rachel, "Rachel, this is Doctor Dean Curtis from the University of Queensland. He is going to be joining us for a short while to share some research with us on the Great Whites."

"Awesome!" Rachel had lost all the final traces of professionalism as she smiled her beaming smile at Dean. "Lucky us!"

Having witnessed enough flirting, Kasie lead Dean through the secured reception door and into her office.

"This is an impressive facility," Dean shared as he entered her large glass office.

"It is indeed," Kasie agreed. "Would you like a tour?" Without waiting for a response, Kasie dropped the contents of her full arms onto her desk and headed for the door. Not needing to spend another second alone in her office with this over-enthusiastic colleague, she thought it best to seek out others with the rationale that there was always safety in numbers.

Having toured the laboratory, the board room, the research centre and shared a coffee or two with the eager staff, Dean was appearing quite at home amongst the walls of the conservation society.

Returning to her office, she left the door ajar while she searched her computer for the photos of Long Island that she had taken just the week before. Pulling the images up on her screen, she began to explain to Dean the important regenerative work of the seagrass the society had managed in order to support the green turtle population. As earlier, Dean had serious, pertinent and informed questions for her.

Their passionate and intelligent conservation discussion was rudely interrupted as the tall, dark man stormed into Kasie's office.

"What the hell are you doing here?" the man demanded of Dean. "I thought I told you to fuck off back to Australia!" he yelled at him.

Dean was on his feet in a shot, not hesitating for a second to stand up to his formidable opponent, "And I told you, that you don't own everyone here and to have some respect," Dean yelled back in his face.

Kasie rushed around the side of her desk and pushed closed her office door to make her way to the two men. Not budging to allow her to fit in between them, she was forced to stand beside them.

"What is this about? Why are you being so incredibly rude?" she demanded of her boss.

"Ask your little friend here," was his only offer of an explanation to the woman he loved.

"Dean?" Kasie turned to her new friend, "What is going on?"

Dean broke his stony stare from the intense man in the room with them. He turned to Kasie. He took her hand and offered up his best explanation, "Your boss here is mad that someone finally had the guts to tell him how it is."

"You don't have a clue what is going on here," her boss abruptly interrupted Dean.

"Stop!" Kasie yelled at him again. She turned her attention once more to Dean. "What are you talking about?"

"The way he treated you the other night Kasie, it wasn't ok. And poor little rich boy here didn't like someone telling him so," Dean went on to explain in more detail.

"I swear..." The dark-haired man exploded before he stopped himself.

Kasie didn't like the explanation she was hearing, nor did she appreciate the way in which her boss had entered the room. She turned to meet his angry, intense green eyes, "We need to talk." She grabbed his hand and led him out of the room. She glanced back at Dean. "Wait here please," she asked him softly.

Kasie walked her boss down the hallway and into the impressive boardroom as she closed and locked the door behind them. He obediently followed her and paused just inside the door for a moment as he watched her turn the small silver lock.

She turned to face him as he reached out, grabbing her waist and pulling her towards him. He leant down to kiss her lips as she raised her palm to his chest, "Stop," she demanded, "Not here… not now!"

"Kase…" he began. "You weren't there, you didn't see what happened, what he said to me. I appreciate you want to work with him, but I am not comfortable with having him here."

"And do you think I was comfortable hearing you minimise our kiss and seeing you with Tiffany?" she replied immediately.

He stopped. His mouth slightly ajar as he paused realising now for the first time the reason behind his lover's vengeful behaviour beside the pool. He suddenly recognised that Kasie had witnessed the inappropriate liaison between him and Tiffany.

"Kase… please let me explain," he began.

"Actually, I don't want an explanation. We are not a couple. You don't have to explain anything to me. You can kiss whomever you want. Hell, you can kiss everyone you want. It doesn't mean anything to me."

He bowed his head, "Kase, please don't say that. I am so sorry. I didn't know what to do. This has all been so difficult, much more than I had ever imagined it would be."

Kasie looked at him confused, "What?" she questioned him. "What does that mean?"

He looked down at her now, his turn to feel confused by her question. He was silent, leaving Kasie to ask the question once more.

"What do you mean when you say, much more than you ever imagined it would be?"

He appeared hesitant to answer, as if trying to understand the purpose behind her questioning, "I'm not sure what you are asking me," he simply stated.

"I'm asking you; how long did you imagine this thing between us would happen?"

"I don't know Kase. It just evolved, I guess. My feelings for you grew the more I got to know you."

Kasie had started to see the bigger picture behind her lover's words. For her this physical attraction, this sexual chemistry between them was a new dynamic in their relationship. She hadn't paused long enough to imagine that it possibly wasn't that new for him. She pieced together some of the clues as to the longevity of his feelings for her. The words spoken to her in his bedroom, telling her he would not let her leave him. His words of love for her, holding within them now a whole new level of intensity.

"So?" she continued on her line of questioning. "Tell me something... The List, was it formed before or after you began to have feelings for me?"

"Kase, I don't know what you are wanting from me?" He tried in vain to avoid the question. He wasn't sure how she might respond if she knew the truth.

"Answer me please. It is a straightforward question." Kasie required an answer. She was surprised by the new information she was hearing and needed to know everything. Piece by piece this puzzle was coming together and she had to view the whole picture to begin to understand how she felt about it all.

He bowed his head and sighed, anticipating maybe that the answer was not going to please his friend.

"Kase, The List was designed with you in mind."

She was shocked. "What?" she demanded to know more. She couldn't understand how this could be possible. The implication of what that meant was enormous.

"Kase, maybe this isn't the time or place for this conversation."

She knew he had a point, but she was now desperate to learn more. "Please explain to me how The List was designed for me."

He began hesitantly to explain as best he could.

"This must be hard to understand, Kase, but it isn't just about women in this town wanting to marry me. It is far more than that. Every family who has lived and worked here alongside mine has earned a part of the town's success. My family just happened to have this vision from the start and therefore gained the most financially from the town and its resources. If there was any way to explain this better, I would. My parents were what you Aussies would consider a king and queen. Their families, were elders, royalty here on the islands. My marriage wasn't ever mine alone to decide upon." He paused, looking at her for reassurance. Her silence suggested he should continue.

"For me to marry someone outside of this island would be like a slap in the face of all those hard-working families who contributed to the town's success. It made sense to everyone that one day one of these families would join us as one of their daughters and I would marry. It was what I was brought up to believe. I always knew that my loyalty to my family's work included an arranged marriage of sorts." He paused as he said the words out loud, "It sounds ridiculous I know."

"It doesn't really, it is very sweet." Kasie's tone softened as she felt for the man pouring his heart out in front of her. She hadn't understood before now the enormity of the pressure his family was under. That he now alone was under, after his parents' death. Having come to this town after the tsunami, she had never had the pleasure of meeting his family and learning for herself the work that they had undertaken. She suddenly felt a little sad at the realisation that she would never get to meet them. She listened with intent as she took in the next crucial pieces of information.

"I knew from the day I met you in this very building, that you were special. The more time we spent together the more my feelings for you grew. I couldn't help what I was feeling but I was also very aware that I had a responsibility to do the right thing by my family. I spoke to Doctor Phoenix about it. Over time he and I developed a plan to introduce the idea of my wife being someone who wasn't born in this town. So, we created the concept of The List."

Kasie began to realise how such a ridiculous concept as The List came to be created.

"When Doctor Phoenix approached me about The List, what would he have done if I had said no to the agreeing to be on it?" Kasie questioned him.

"I guess we hadn't thought that far ahead. I was hoping that maybe you were beginning to feel the same way about me. We got along so well and you were always at the house with Marco and I. So, I hoped that you were starting to fall in love with me too."

Kasie reflected back to those cozy nights at the mansion, watching indie movies cuddled up to her friend on the couch. Playing pool with him and Marco, having lots of laughs. She tried to recall her emotions at the time. She remembered that she always thought her friend was unbelievably gorgeous and sexy.

She knew she openly flirted with him as he did with her. She recalled Marco always joking about being the third wheel, although she really didn't give much thought as to why. His idea of The List, as ludicrous as it had sounded from the beginning was starting to make some sense, but there was still something troubling her.

"This still doesn't explain why you told Tiffany that our kiss meant nothing and why you proceeded to lead her on," Kasie continued her questioning.

"I can't explain that. I guess I have been trying so hard to pretend like nothing was happening that I just remained in that role." He looked at Kasie, a very serious and sincere tone in his voice. "You know when… I mean… if, you decide that you want to be with me too, I will make that announcement to the town immediately. No more pretenses, just you and me together. People will have to deal with that in whatever way they can."

He reflected before adding, "Including your little admirer there in the other room." Another pause before he added again, "It killed me watching you kiss him. Did I mention that?" He pouted as he searched her face for some sympathy.

"Well I didn't enjoy either of the Tiffany shows myself. Did I mention that?" she mimicked him.

"I'm sorry." He leant in to kiss her face and this time she didn't stop him. "It will never happen again."

She was conscious of making Dean wait and she let her boss know he needed to leave. Walking him back through the hallway, they passed her office just as Dean was opening her office door.

"See ya, mate!" Dean yelled out at his competition as he watched him head for the exit.

Kasie paused by Dean's side, hoping that her boss would continue exiting without incident.

Without missing a stride, the two Australians watched as the handsome dark-haired man continued toward the exit, lifting one hand in the air to wave goodbye. Not turning around, he replied with a heavy tone of sarcasm in his voice. "No, see you mate, cause I'm not going anywhere!"

Dean turned to Kasie, "How can you stand working for that man?"

"Well, it's complicated," she replied.

"Yeah," Dean agreed. "I keep hearing that."

SEVENTEEN

THE GAOL

Dean and Kasie continued sharing their research findings and stories of life back home well into the early evening. "How about we head out for a drink?" Dean suggested at the end of the long day.

Agreeing that the idea was a valid one, Kasie sent a quick text to Dee. She turned to Dean and suggested her plan, "How about we head out to The Gaol? You will love it, it is an old converted Gaol, closed down decades ago, but it has the best atmosphere. It is the place in town to go for a cocktail. I will need to go home and get changed though, and pick up Dee. I can meet you there," Kasie suggested.

"Sounds great, how about nine o'clock?" Dean agreed.

"Sounds like a perfect idea."

True to his word, Dean was showered, dressed and looking drop dead gorgeous arriving at The Gaol at precisely nine o'clock. Dressed in a casual pair of blue jeans and dark brown boots, topped off with a very tight-fitting linen button up shirt, displaying just the perfect amount of exposure to his tanned, muscular chest.

Dee and Kasie, who now seemed to make a habit of it, were running late yet again. They pulled into the car park of The Gaol roughly twenty minutes after the agreed meeting time, the two women alighted the vehicle to be greeted by their sexy companion.

"Must be your shout first for keeping me waiting," Dean joked with the women.

Taking his time now to further explore both women with his eyes, he decided he had changed his mind. "On second thoughts, my shout, the wait was worth every second."

Dee giggled at their friend's flirty comments. The three of them turned and began making their way to the lift. Pulling her friend's arm so that they were a step behind their sexy companion, Dee whispered into her friend's ear.

"Is it possible that he is just a blonde version of Prince Charming?"

Kasie giggled at the thought. "God, I hope not!" Both women knew there could be only one royal bachelor and that the island itself wasn't large enough to handle any more than one.

As they made their way up the lift and into the crowded bar, Kasie smiled and greeted the familiar faces of several of the party guests from the previous night. Introducing Dean to a few of the guys, she was pleased that they seemed much less threatened by the hunky tourist than her guest in her office earlier that day. Not hearing, but feeling her phone vibrate in her bag, Kasie reached for it to check her text messages.

There was one from her boss:

Hey Kase, wondering if you would like some company tonight? xx

She thought it best if she replied immediately:

Sorry, I'm not at home. I'm out with friends at The Gaol. Xx

His reply was instant:

Does one of them look like a discarded hippy surfer from the 70s? You might recognise him from his arrogant attitude and obnoxious accent. xx

She laughed at his bitchiness:

Jealousy really doesn't suit you! And he would probably say exactly the same thing about you, but yes, Dean is here along with Dee. ☺ xx

Another instant reply:

I'm on my way xx

Kasie found Dee's face in the crowd. She pouted at her, pulling a face as if to suggest that she had done something incredibly stupid. She lifted her phone in the air to further explain her contact.

Dee couldn't read the message but could guess at what had just transpired. She shook her head and let out a sigh. It was going to be another interesting night in Coral Cove, she thought to herself. But at least she would get to see Marco again. She secretly hoped that he would accompany his friend to The Gaol to check up on Kasie.

The three friends had only just purchased their second round of drinks, when the doors of the elevator opened and all eyes turned to witness the sought-after bachelor himself walk into the busy room. Followed as always by his faithful friend, Marco.

The two men walked past their fellow guests, saying quick hellos and kisses with the girls and handshakes or pats on the back with the guys. They made a beeline toward Kasie, Dee and Dean.

Both men walked straight up to the girls and planted a kiss on each of them before they turned their attention to Dean. Offering his hand in greeting, the bachelor remarked, "We seem to be sharing the unpleasant experience of bumping into each other a bit lately."

Dean laughed, not accepting his hand, instead rising from his seat to say, "I'm not exactly pleased to see you here either. But I am getting the distinct impression that you are not here to see me anyway." He turned his attention to his female companions. "My gorgeous girls, I might say goodnight so this doesn't turn into another unpleasant experience for all of us."

Dean began to step away from the group when Kasie grabbed his bulging bicep. "No Dean. Don't go. We came here for a drink. Please stay."

She turned her attention to her boss, still standing, hands now in his pockets, looking extremely unhappy with the direction the conversation was going. "And you can stay as long as you promise to stop being a jealous brat. I am here with my friends for drinks, you are welcome to join us, as long as you remain hospitable!"

The tall, dark man looked at Kasie and smiled, "You are the only person I know who could say that to me and still make me smile. You are correct, as always. I am finding being in this particular Aussie's company very difficult. I will leave you to be. Have a great night. I'll talk to you tomorrow." He leant forward and kissed her lips. "And Dee…" he bent down and kissed her on the cheek, "you look simply gorgeous as always."

He turned his attention to Dean. "Sorry mate, I'll have to run," he said as he offered his hand once more.

Dean still standing moved one step closer to the man, allowing his outstretched hand to be crushed by Dean's ripped, hard stomach. "No thank you mate," Dean said with heavy sarcasm. "And if you offer me that hand one more time, I am likely to crush it."

"Down boy!" His opponent was quick witted with his response. Not shirking for a moment, he simply smiled into the eyes of his competition.

The tall, dark man turned once more to Dee. "Look after her!" he instructed as he motioned towards Kasie.

Dean gained the bachelor's attention once more and spoke sternly and directly at him. "She is not your fucking possession mate!"

"And she is not yours either Dean!"

"Enough boys!" Kasie interrupted. "I am quickly tiring of you both, you should see yourselves right now, work this stuff out or you can both leave."

"It's ok, I'm going," her boss replied and turned to head for the exit.

He had only walked a step or two when he heard from behind him, "Yeah, see you mate, cause I'm not going anywhere." Dean showed no fear of the man who owned the town. He knew how to stand his ground and he had no reason to feel intimidated by anyone, let alone this arrogant narcissist who appeared to have everyone wrapped around his little finger.

Only a few steps away, Marco looked at his boss, the rage in his eyes like he had only seen one time before. It was the night they arrived at this very spot, in The Gaol, to find Kasie there with Doctor Chris. Marco nudged his boss to the exit with some gentle words of encouragement.

Once the two men had disappeared into the crowd, Dean returned to his seat next to the girls. "Honestly Kasie, what is going on between you and him?"

"It's complicated," was all she could say in response to Dean's valid concern for her. She really didn't want to explain anything more at the moment and if she was honest with herself, she was having some very contradictory thoughts about their current relationship status. She knew she still loved her friend, but she was finding his current behaviour and the complexity of the situation with The List extremely challenging.

"Go ahead and un-complicate it for me then. Tell me all about it. Cause from where I stand, you deserve a lot better than that possessive, jealous rich twat."

"Oh twat, that is a strong word. You do know what that means, don't you Dean?" Dee laughed.

"I know exactly what that word means and I was trying to be gentlemanly and not use the Australian version of the word to describe your friend there."

He turned to Kasie once more, "Please enlighten me, what is going on between you and him? Are you a couple? Were you a couple?"

"No, nothing like that," Kasie began to explain. "We just, we have just had a bit of a thing I guess."

"So, is it over?" Dean enquired.

"Well, it never really got started," Kasie explained further.

Seeming relieved that was the extent of their relationship, Dean turned his attention once more to the two women, "Where were we? Before we were rudely interrupted that is?" he joked. "Oh yes, here's to us!" He glanced first to Dee and then with a lingering stare, toasted Kasie, sexily adding a playful wink.

What could have turned into a disaster given their unexpected visitor, turned out to be one of the best nights out Kasie and Dee could remember. Laughing and dancing and drinking, the three Aussies let loose and enjoyed their common homeland stories and in-house jokes. Like giddy primary school kids, they designed a secret handshake and laughed at its increasing degree of difficulties with each added manouvre.

Dee was quickly becoming the centre of attention as she took to the dancefloor with her previous evening's pool partners. Watching her spin around the floor dancing and laughing with each of the men, Kasie suddenly realised what had been absent in her life most recently.

"You know what? This place can feel stifling," she explained out of the blue to Dean.

"Yeah, I can see that. Especially with your, what do they call him, Prince Charming?" He scoffed as the words left his mouth. "Having him watching over you like a hawk, swooping down every time he sees you having too much fun, like the dark shadow of gloom over your otherwise sunny disposition."

"Dean, you are so funny, that is the most hilarious description I have ever heard of him."

"I have more if you like," he offered up.

"No thanks. I am sure I will hear the rest sooner or later. Tell me, why do you dislike him so much?" Kasie questioned him.

Dean thought about the answer. Not taking her question lightly he pondered before responding, "I guess I have just known guys like him. My little sister was dating a guy similar to him. He tried to take all her freedom away, restricted her going out and who she spent time with. It was really concerning."

"And then what happened?" Kasie was on the edge of her seat waiting to hear if her story had a happy ending.

He smiled at Kasie. "Well then big brother stepped in of course." He paused while she searched her mind for what that might mean, "It's all good. She is with someone who treats her really well now. I think he is planning to propose soon actually."

"You have a big family?"

"Yeah, two sisters, a brother, mum and dad. All living on either the Gold Coast or in Brisbane. No one moved too far away. All married or about to get married, except me. Unlucky last." He brought his hands to his face as if to wipe away a tear.

"Oh no, so sad." Kasie draped the sarcasm thickly over her words. "I'm sure that won't be the case for long. There are a dozen girls in this room alone, who look like they would like the chance to get to know you."

"Really?" he joked as he pretended to stand up and search the room. Placing his straight palm to meet the line of his eyebrows, he turned his head slightly left and then slightly right.

Kasie laughed again. She couldn't believe how easy it was to be around Dean. "I think I know what I have been missing."

"What?" Dean asked excitedly.

"Fun!" Kasie yelled with glee back at him. "Fun, laughter, lightness," she added.

Dean wasted no time in obliging her, standing from his seat he stood in front of her, offering his hand as if to dance, "Well, I am here to offer my services."

Kasie jumped up, grabbed his hand with hers and dragged him on to the dancefloor. They made their way to where Dee was holding court and the three of them began once more laughing and dancing the night away.

Finally, after several long hours, the night drew to a close. "Goodnight my gorgeous girls," Dean offered a kiss on the cheek for them both as they stood in the car park about to step into their vehicles.

"Goodnight Dean," the two girls chimed in unison.

"Sweet dreams," he added.

Dean turned back to Kasie, as if just remembering something he had forgotten. "Hey Kasie, do you think I could stop by your office again tomorrow? There is something I need to talk to you about."

"Oh, that sounds interesting," Kasie giggled.

"Yeah, it is actually pretty important. Is that ok?"

"Of course, Dean," Kasie added without hesitation. "See you tomorrow."

In the car, the girls began to debrief the night. "Dean is so much fun," Dee observed.

"Maybe the two of you could catch up when you both return home?" Kasie suggested.

"Yeah maybe we could have a drink and he could sit there all night asking me questions about you. What's her favourite colour? What kind of music does she like? Does she like anyone we know?"

Kasie roared with laughter. "You make it sound like we are back in high school again."

"That is what it feels like, standing back and watching two guys literally fight over you."

"Don't be ridiculous Dee. Dean isn't at all interested in me in any romantic kind of a way. We just get along. We have lots in common and we laugh together."

"Oh yeah, how stupid of me to imagine that would be any kind of a basis for a long and happy relationship," she laughed a sarcastic over-the-top laugh to further illustrate her sarcasm.

"Seriously, if you can't see that gorgeous hunk of a surf-god isn't completely smitten with you, you need to open your eyes," she continued.

"I think you are reading too much into this Dee. He was telling me tonight that he compared my boss to his little sister's ex-boyfriend. I think meeting him just triggered a negative reaction to him. It doesn't have anything to do with me."

"Really? And what about your handsome boss? How can you explain his jealous outbursts of late?"

"Yeah, well, he is just acting like a possessive boyfriend, which can I remind everyone he isn't," Kasie answered her friend.

"Kasie, listen to what you are saying." Dee continued, "Prince Charming would only need to act like a possessive, jealous boyfriend if he perceived a threat. He is the perfect friend to every other male in Coral Cove. The only time I have ever seen him act this way is when he thought his little Kasie was falling under the spell of another man. Just think about it."

Kasie didn't really want to think about it. She didn't want to admit that the comparisons between Dean's story of his little sister and her were at the moment eerily similar. She really wasn't enjoying her boss's jealous outbursts. Sure, maybe at first, at the party when he kissed her, his mention of punishment for making him jealous was a bit of a turn on. And his promise to not let her leave his bedroom was a sign for Kasie of just how intense his feelings for her had become.

But Dean was right and so was Dee. He was acting like a jealous, possessive boyfriend and he had no right to do so. But did she act any differently when she saw him kiss Tiffany? She behaved just as badly, pulling poor Dean into this twisted mess that was her life. What was it with men? For years, she barely had a date and then all of a sudden, this onslaught of men acting possessive of her, first her boss, then Doctor Chris and now Dean. Kasie couldn't understand why her life had suddenly become so complicated.

EIGHTEEN

THE GREAT WHITE SHARKS

The morning after began as any other. Kasie made her first coffee and a mental list of tasks for the day while Dee slept in. Arriving at work, Kasie was actually looking forward to speaking to Dean again to find out what this important information he wanted to share with her was.

She was relieved to find that he wasn't waiting for her in reception as she had some urgent tasks to complete before he arrived. Kasie greeted Rachel as she entered and feeling a little cheeky decided to tell her that she was expecting Dean Curtis again and to let him in when he arrived.

Rachel smiled a wide smile and immediately reached into her handbag to find a mirror and lip gloss for a quick reapplication. Kasie walked toward the security-coded door.

"Oh," Rachel offered, "I nearly forgot to tell you, the boss is here. Having some meeting or something," she added.

Clearly, Kasie thought to herself, Rachel must be the one single woman in town who doesn't melt every time their boss walked into the room. But she did smile to think of how much Rachel looked like she enjoyed flirting with the gorgeous Dean.

Kasie thanked Rachel and proceeded cautiously toward her office. She took a deep breath and opened her door. There as she suspected was her boss. There he was, her very own lover waiting in her guest chair for her imminent arrival.

"I didn't know we had a meeting scheduled for this morning," she began as she walked in through the door.

"I'm sorry, I didn't know I needed to book in an appointment to see you," he offered as a way of apology.

"I don't mean to sound rude, but I have a lot on today," she continued.

"I'm sorry, I won't keep you," he apologised again as he began to exit the room.

She looked at him and felt instantly guilty for her cold treatment of him. "Wait, I'm sorry too," she said, "I guess I am a little pissed at you still."

"Well, I probably deserve that." He turned to face her. "Will you forgive me for my inexcusably bad behaviour of last night?"

She looked him in the eyes. His deep, green eyes and gorgeous smile still having that undeniable effect on her. "Of course," she walked toward him to offer him a friendly hug.

"No kiss?" he cheekily asked.

"No, not in the workplace," she instantly replied. "Can you please just explain to me, what is your problem with Dean? He is actually a really nice guy."

"I can see that you and him must share a lot in common. I just don't trust the guy. I don't like him and I don't like him constantly in your presence."

"He isn't constantly in my presence," Kasie defended herself.

On cue, her phone rang. Kasie answered and listened to the short message for her. "Thanks Rachel, you can let him in."

Her boss stood before her, taking a lucky guess at who the visitor was being sent to her office at this precise moment. "What did you say about him not always being constantly in your presence?" he asked. "I have barely had five minutes alone with you for days," he pleaded. "And every time I get close to you, he turns up."

"Well if I remember correctly, part of the reason for that, was your desire to get up close and personal with a certain woman named Tiffany."

Dean chose that exact moment to walk in the door. "Well, look who's here again," Dean commented with sarcasm as he entered Kasie's office.

"Ah yes, you again," her boss retorted. "Tell me, I know you work with marine ecology, but in Australia, isn't there an insect that attaches itself to a person and is nearly impossible to remove?"

"Dean, you don't have to answer that," Kasie pleaded with him. She could see exactly what her boss was alluding to.

"No, it's ok, I am all for education of those less fortunate," He replied to Kasie. Dean was not in the least bit intimidated by the brooding billionaire who was Kasie's boss.

He turned to his tall, dark counterpart, "Well actually, there is something called a paralysis tick, deadly to animals like dogs and cats. It is a small grey coloured insect. It attaches to the skin and starts burrowing in, feeding on blood as it engorges itself. Almost impossible to remove without breaking it in half and once disturbed it can discharge a poison that can paralyze an animal and kill it, if left untreated," Dean educated his nemesis with a wide, smug grin on his face.

He added one final comment, "Urban legend has it that a large enough one could possess enough poison to even kill a rich, arrogant, annoying brat just like yourself. If it happened to chance upon one, one day, that is," Dean laughed at his own insult.

"And how would one rid themselves of this annoying paralysis tick?" Her boss seemingly unfazed by the earlier insult continued to question Dean.

"Oh well, that is just it, once it has entered too far under the person's skin, the damage is done. Even if it is removed, it has already made its mark. Sorry I couldn't offer you any better news."

"No, thanks Dean, you have given me all the information I needed." He began to walk out the door, "Oh and by the way, did I mention I own a private jet? I would be more than happy to offer you a lift home to Australia in comfort, if you would like. I could have it ready in less than an hour," he added hopefully.

"Well, thank you, old man, that is very generous of you, but I actually have my own plane to catch, the day after tomorrow," Dean replied. "Very important things to get back home to," he added. "Which is why I needed to talk to you Kasie, before I leave." Turning his full attention to Kasie, Dean paused for effect. He knew just how to anger her boss and he wasn't letting up anytime soon.

Choosing not to take the bait, the tall, dark boss upon leaving the room turned one last time to Kasie, "Dinner tomorrow night Kase?" His tone was light and hopeful. "Your place maybe or at the mansion if you are more comfortable there?"

Kasie shot daggers at her boss, "I will let you know, thanks for the invite." She motioned for him to close the door behind himself as he left.

Kasie wondered if it was wrong to feel slightly turned on by the possibility of these two gorgeous men fighting over her. She didn't want to believe it but they appeared to be spelling it out for each other.

It was as if they were two of a kind in very different bodies fighting for their woman. Kind of sexy, Kasie thought to herself. And as long as it wasn't coming to blows in her office, she could put up with the few minor jabs and insults.

Once they were alone Kasie turned to Dean, "So, what is this important news?" She was keen to hear what Dean was so anxious to tell her.

"I assume you have heard of the plight of the sharks in Western Australia?"

"Yes, oh my god, it is sickening, I can't bear to see the images of those poor sharks being shot in the head and dragged beside the boat. What is the Western Australian government thinking in allowing this to happen? How did this all start?"

"Well, there were unfortunately some recent tragic deaths in the water due to sharks. They hadn't confirmed for sure if it was a Great White or several Great Whites or something completely different. The government seems relentless. They have placed baited hooks and nets off the coastline in an attempt to kill the sharks. They haven't caught any yet, but they have killed hundreds of tiger sharks in the process, many have been young sharks as well."

"It is so sad, is there anything we can do?" Kasie questioned him.

Dean smiled his wide, cheeky grin at her, "I am glad you asked."

Kasie felt nervous at what was about to be said.

Dean continued, "I wasn't going to ask you this, but now that I have met you and I just had confirmation late yesterday afternoon that this was going ahead. I was hoping there might be a chance that you could testify, that is be one of our scientific experts in our legal fight against the government's legislation. I don't think that they could offer to pay you. I am doing it out of principle but the conservation society leading the challenge might be able to pay for your airfare."

Kasie laughed, "There is always the private jet you were offered."

"Yeah, as if I would hop on that. He would probably secretly sabotage it just so I didn't make it home." Dean paused, "Does that mean you will do it? Come back to Australia and testify with me?" He looked hopefully at her. Raising his hands in prayer, he grinned and got down on his knees before her and begged, "Please?"

I'll think about it. I would have to get time away from here, so I would have to ask my boss."

Dean interrupted her, "And he can't join us, if that is what he suggests to you as a compromise."

Kasie corrected him, "Of course not. There is no way I would want to be on the same plane as you and him together. I am pretty sure the universe would find some way of creating the worst turbulence it could ever create, just to give you some justice for your bad behaviour."

"So, what do you think he would say? Would he give you the time off?" Dean asked with growing excitement.

"Well, I guess he doesn't really have a choice, as much as I like to call him my boss, I am only a contractor here and really could leave whenever I want."

"Kasie, I cannot thank you enough, I will ring them straight away and have them book your flight. You can travel home with me the day after tomorrow. Keep me company. We can work on our statements together on the plane."

Dean turned to leave the room but had to stop a moment to share an exciting new thought that had just occurred to him. He had thoroughly enjoyed getting to know Kasie and imagined there might be some chance he could find a way to spend a lot more time with her. "You never know, once you go home, you may decide to stay… there… with me?" he suggested with a sexy hint of something very alluring.

Dean walked from Kasie's office and into the hallway and immediately sensed someone's eyes on him. He turned to see the tall dark-haired man leering at him from the entrance to the boardroom. Dean realised that the jealous billionaire was obviously waiting for him to leave to return to his interrupted conversation with Kasie.

From inside the office, now having returned to her desk, Kasie said goodbye again to Dean. She was happy to let him see himself out. He was beginning to find his way around and it would also give Rachel on reception a chance at a little time to flirt with him.

Dean glanced toward Kasie and then back to her boss. "See you!" Dean replied, loud enough for the onlooker to hear. "See you at the airport, if not before," he smiled at her. He closed her office door and looked back one last time. He checked to make sure his message was heard loud and clear. There standing in the hallway was his nemesis, looking like he was about to leap forth and attack Dean.

Not worrying for a minute about his personal safety, Dean smiled and waved at him, turned toward the exit and headed out the front door.

Just when Kasie thought her excitement for the day was over and she could peacefully get started on her to-do list, her office door abruptly opened. She looked up to see her boss standing in her doorway, white as a sheet.

"No knocking now either?" she playfully joked with him.

Obviously not here for pleasantries, he led in with his questioning straight away, "Please tell me you aren't thinking of hopping on a plane with that arrogant twat?"

Kasie laughed at his dramatic phrasing, "How funny, I think he called you the same thing last night while we were having drinks at The Gaol."

"Kase?" Her boss was all business as he walked toward her. He needed an immediate answer to his question. "Please tell me you aren't catching a plane anywhere with that guy?"

"Look," she began to explain herself. "This isn't the place for this conversation. How about I get some work done and come over to your place after that. We can talk about it then."

Thinking that was exactly what the two of them needed he was pleased with the compromise and readily agreed. "Fine, I will ask Helen to make us some dinner. You can have the spare room, if you would like to stay." He smiled at her as another idea entered his head, "Or you could bring your toothbrush and stay with me?" he added hopefully.

"Dinner sounds lovely but there will be no sleepovers!" Kasie instructed him.

"Ok," he put his palms up to surrender. This battle obviously lost. "But just so you know, the offer always stands, anytime."

"Thanks, I feel confident that if I ever need somewhere to sleep for the night, that you would be kind enough to offer me a spare bed."

"Or at least half a bed," he flirted back at her not so innocently.

Kasie watched her second guest of the morning exit the office and head for the reception area. She hoped that Rachel hadn't kept Dean for too long and that the men would both exit the reception and the car park without further incident. Even with the distractions, Kasie managed to enjoy a productive workday. She went home, showered and changed and made her way to the mansion. She was surprised to see the usual array of security and staff cars missing. She walked up the grand stairs to the huge, imposing front door. As she raised her hand to tap on the impressive entry she was greeted by her host as he opened the door for her.

"Please Kase, you never need to knock, I am hoping you begin to see this as your home. Come and go as you please."

"Thanks," was all she could think to say as a reply. She was feeling slightly nervous about the quietness of the mansion. "Where is everyone?" Kasie asked.

"I have given everyone the night off. I thought it was important that we were alone tonight."

Kasie could feel her stomach turn at the thought of what was yet to come. "Where is Marco?" she added for further clarification as to what alone actually meant.

"To be honest I think he is with Dee," her host explained.

Feeling slightly uneasy with the two of them alone in the mansion, Kasie was quick to clarify the reason for her visit, "Actually I probably need to tell you this visit is more business than pleasure tonight."

His face looked suddenly concerned. She could tell he was trying his best to remain unconcerned. "Would you like a drink?" he offered, ever the gracious host.

"Sure," Kasie agreed before she followed him into the main lounge area on the lower level. What greeted her was a picnic of sorts, a lavish array of foods, drinks and treats laid out before them on a large, red picnic blanket.

Kasie could only imagine that her boss had some inkling as to the reason behind her visit. He did after all hear Dean's teasing words, like a threat to her friend that she was about to leave him. Feeling the tension between them and eager not to disappoint her lovely host, Kasie spoke again, "Do you think I can just blurt out what I came here to tell you?"

"I have a feeling I am not going to like it either way, so I guess… yes… go ahead."

Kasie took a deep breath and then began, "I want to ask you as my boss, if I could take some time off," Kasie began.

His face lightened at hearing the request. "Yes, of course, Kase, you don't need to ask me that, your schedule is your own to work out how you please. You can come and go as you wish. You don't even need to check in with me."

She interrupted him mid-sentence, "Good, because I am going back to Australia for a short trip to help with a shark conservation issue they are having there in Western Australia."

Her boss replied quickly. Appearing not in the least bit shocked by what he had just heard, she knew he had guessed already. "I applaud you for offering your help Kase. It is a ridiculous and cruel legislation that they have implemented." He paused thoughtfully for a moment, before he added, "But are you going back with him?"

"Yes," she replied without hesitation. She likened it to ripping off an elastic plaster. She just wanted to get this done as quickly and as painlessly as possible.

She watched as her friend slowly walked toward her. He had digested the information painfully as he poured the two of them a glass of white wine each. "Is there more you want to tell me?" he asked with complete control in his voice.

"More? Anything in particular you are referring to when you ask for more?" Kasie prompted him, feeling uncertain about what his line of questioning was leading to.

"I am asking you if you have feelings for that jackass?" His composure and calm had left him now as he allowed his raw feelings to surface. He looked vulnerable, childlike almost as his jealousy took hold of him once more. This very primal emotion within him was strong and never far from the surface.

Kasie laughed, "You are normally so proper, maybe even overly formal and then when it comes to insulting Dean, you regress to the emotional maturity of a young child. Dean is not a jackass. He is a lovely guy who is just passionate about his work. The same as I am." Kasie felt her anger grow as she attempted to defend her new friend to her old one.

Her boss continued, "Kase, you should know you are a beautiful and intelligent woman."

"Ok," she hesitated, not quite understanding where he was going with his latest comment.

"But I don't think it is your brain that Dean is interested in," he continued.

Kasie jumped up from the lounge she had just settled into, "How absolutely disgusting of you to suggest such a thing. Dean is asking me to give so-called expert testimony in the legal fight against the Western Australian government and their horrific legislation. Dean isn't after my body. He is asking me to come to Australia for my research and experience in the area of shark conservation."

Kasie was furious. She placed her untouched wine glass down on the nearest table and began to make her way from the room and back into the grand entrance.

She stopped momentarily to continue to voice her disappointment in her host, "Really, your jealousy knows no bounds does it? And it isn't an attractive quality at all. Let me assure you of that!"

She continued to make her way from the lounge area growing more furious with each step, "How insulting of you to suggest that I couldn't offer an intelligent argument in this debate." She was working herself into a frenzy, "How horrendous of you to say such a thing!"

Not wanting to spend another second in his company, Kasie picked up speed and bounded toward the door.

Her friend raced behind her eager to catch up before she left the house altogether, "Wait Kase!" he pleaded with her. "I'm so sorry, I didn't mean it like that. Everything I say lately is coming out wrong. Please wait, please let me explain."

"No!" Kasie responded. "I don't want to hear your explanation. I don't' want to hear another word from you tonight! This is all too hard." She felt the tears well up in her eyes. She paused. The emotion was washing over her like an enormous wave crashing over her head, over and over again. She hoped she hadn't said too much. "I'm sorry," she began. "Please," she begged him as the tears began to fall.

Sensing her torment, he reached for her and wrapped his familiar arms around her. He kissed her on the top of her head as he pulled her into him.

"Shh," he whispered to her. "Please don't cry. I didn't mean to hurt you. Please don't leave us like this."

They stood there, silent for a long while, her sobbing into his chest. Him, kissing her and trying to reassure her with his words, "Everything is going to be ok. I'm so sorry. Please don't go," he repeated over and over to her.

She was vaguely listening to his words instead focused on enjoyed the warm, comfortable feel of his embrace.

"Kase," he finally released her as his eyes found hers. He reached for her face and wiped a tear from her cheek. "I am sorry, please forgive me. I never meant to hurt you." He was being honest with her. He hadn't meant to hurt her as much as he had lately. He felt such intense emotions at times and his jealousy was out of control. He guessed the abductions and the fear of losing her were having an effect on him and causing him to behave in ways he would never have imagined possible before.

Kasie looked at the man she loved. She felt overwhelmed at the feelings she had held back. She had been finding it difficult with the merry-go-round of highs and lows she had been experiencing. It all boiled to the top and erupted in one teary, painful mess of tangled words and emotions. She felt her heart tear in two as she whispered the words to him.

"Us," she paused, "it shouldn't hurt this much."

The words came rushing out before she had time to consider their effects. The emotions were too much to bear. The words were true, until now only ever uttered in the dark, silent recess of her mind, she now allowed them to filter through rushing from her mouth, causing in that moment both a much-needed release and a heartbreaking pain.

Kasie released herself from his strong arms and made her way through the front door. She didn't look in his direction as she pushed open the heavy door. She felt the need to turn back one last time to reassure him, "I leave the day after tomorrow, but I will be back."

NINETEEN

THE FLIGHT HOME

The next two days were filled with finishing off necessary reports, coordinating staff to check on tasks in her absence and packing enough clothes to last for what she imagined might be a two or three week stay. Her ever faithful friend, Dee had agreed to join the pair on their flight back home and packed all of her own belongings assuming she wouldn't be returning to Coral Cove, at least not anytime soon.

Kasie checked her watch once more wondering when Dee would return home and hoping it was in time to get to the airport and catch their plane. She heard the front door of her little house open and then quickly close and she rushed to check on her friend.

"Dee?" she called to her from her bedroom. Receiving no response, she walked into the lounge room to find her friend slumped onto her huge blue and white sofa. "Dee, are you ok?" she asked her weary looking friend.

Dee looked up at her, "Kase, that man of yours, he is a mess. It's as if you are leaving him for good, not just going away for a couple of weeks. I swear if he asked me one more time when you were flying back, I was going to strangle him. Why couldn't you just agree to say goodbye to him before you flew out?"

"I couldn't Dee. I just needed to have a clear head and focus on getting my work in order and begin preparing the materials I need for my testimony. I will see him soon enough."

"But will you? From the little I could gather from him and Marco, he fears you may not come back. He didn't say it but from what Marco and he were suggesting, I think they are both of the opinion you are leaving Coral Cove for a life in Australia with Dean."

"Well you and I both know that is not happening, I am just helping Dean out with a very worthy cause I might add. I can sort everything out with Marco and the others when I return."

"I don't know how you can be so calm," Dee added. "I feel like I have just been interrogated by Scotland Yard."

"I'm so sorry Dee, I didn't mean for you to face the brunt of their questions. I will text them both and say goodbye and remind them that I will be back."

As promised, Kasie paused as she thought about the right words to use. Her first text was to Marco:

Hey Marco, flying out soon, will miss you!
Take care of our friend until I return!!! ☺ xx

His reply was equally concise:

You will owe me for this! Look after yourself!
And hurry up and get back or I will fly to Australia myself and bring you
back!!! ☹ xx

Kasie giggled to herself at Marco's response. Now for the difficult one:

Hey you, I'm leaving soon, just wanted to say goodbye
And I will see you soon. I promise! xx

His reply was but a few words:

I love you! Xx

Kasie couldn't respond to the words in front of her. She wasn't able to yet again. She knew she loved this man, but she didn't know if that love was good for her or causing her more pain than she could bear. She figured that she had said goodbye and she would work the rest out when she got back. Kasie grabbed her bags and her best friend and made her way to the airport.

The flight home was a lot of fun. More fun actually than she could ever remember having on a plane. Time with Dee and Dean was always enjoyable, always light she thought to herself. It was a nice change from the drama of her life recently. The pilot announced their descent into Cairns airport. A quick stopover in Cairns before driving the hour and a half to Port Douglas to drop Dee home and make a short visit to her parents.

Spending a day or two with family and friends was just what Kasie needed right now. She planned to do some work with Dean and slip in some time to prepare their statements for court before flying off together to Perth to meet with the other delegates and legal representative, to prepare the overall case against the Western Australian Government's legislation.

"Are you ready to meet the family?" Kasie asked Dean.

"A little earlier in the relationship than I would normally like to do it, but what the hell," he joked with her.

Dee poked a pointy elbow into Kasie's ribs. Glancing over she saw Dee's arched brows. She recognised her close-lipped smile as she was indicating that she too heard the flirty remark from the gorgeous man sitting beside her friend.

Kasie's memories of Dee scanned back to when they were best friends in high school. Joined at the hip, was how people often described the two friends. Dee appeared to be interested in only one thing in high school… boys, while Kasie enjoyed the study and the competition with the guys to see who could get the best marks in the class.

Kasie remembered her arch nemesis in her grade, a nerdy looking, greasy haired boy called Derek. He reveled in the short-lived attention every time a teacher shared the marks with the class, with him always making it to top of the list.

She remembered looking over at his smug face and thinking how nice it would be to beat him, at least once. It became Kasie's obsession during her final years of secondary school to get the better mark, to be able to look smugly over at Derek and know that she had beaten him, even if it was only once.

Intelligence, she thought to herself, that is the sexiest quality in a man, and humour. The right combination of sexy, funny and smart made the perfect man for her. Dee on the other hand, as she remembered back to high school always preferred the sporty guys, the guys with the muscles and the raw athleticism.

Kasie guessed that was why she was so enthralled by Marco, sexy, strong and athletic. Marco's body was a fit, lean and muscular fighting machine, or so she had remembered from Dee's description of it.

She chose to prefer to not think of her good friend in that way. Smart, sexy and funny Kasie thought again to herself. She wondered if that was why she found herself increasingly drawn to the blonde man sitting beside her.

The plane landed and their gentlemanly companion managed to find all of their luggage from the carousel and load it expertly on the trolley before Dee and Kasie even realised it had arrived. Busy greeting their family who had arrived at the airport to pick them up, Kasie was overwhelmed by the emotion of seeing her loved ones again in person.

"Three years," her father kept repeating to her, "three years you were gone!"

"She said one year. One year!" her mother added each time. "One year she said she would be gone." She wondered where the reset button was to reboot her parents out of their perpetual loop.

Dee's mother approached her next, "Are you ok my dear? Dee was so worried about you, she had to just rush to your side."

"I'm ok Auntie Gwyneth, but please just keep it down in front of my parents," Kasie pleaded.

"Of course, dear," Dee's mother agreed. "You still haven't told them?"

"No," Kasie whispered. "No need to worry them now about it, is there?" she asked Gwyneth hopefully.

"No, of course not dear. Welcome home love," she added.

Kasie had loved her best friend's mother as her own. She was a gentle and warm soul. A trusted confidant. When growing up, Kasie didn't feel she could talk to her own mother, especially when it came to boys. Gwyneth had been much more casual and laidback and happy to talk relationships with the girls on their nights sleeping over at Dee's house. And her advice was solid. As Kasie grew older she often found herself drawing on Gwyneth's advice, remembering her clear and well-thought-through words on how a man should treat a woman he loved.

Kasie wondered if she should seek out Gwyneth once more, maybe use her as a sounding board of sorts to try to sort through some of the opposing thoughts she was having about her impending relationship with her employer.

Kasie kissed Dee's mother on the cheek and turned her attention back to her own mother and father. Seeing Dean approach her father, hand outstretched, her mother, eyes wide open, mesmerised by the Adonis before her, Kasie raced forward to intercept the introductions.

"Good morning sir, I am Dean Curtis, a friend of your daughter and Dee's. It is lovely to meet you both."

Kasie was so grateful to Dean for clearing up any misconceptions straight away and wanted to give him some extra brownie points for his thoughtfulness.

"That is Doctor Dean Curtis, Mum," Kasie teased, knowing full well that the word doctor would be music to her mother's ears.

"Oh, a doctor?" Kasie's mother's voice went up an octave. "A friend of both of the girls?" her voice continuing to rise to insane levels that only dogs could hear.

"Yes Mum, Dean is a friend of ours, I was hoping he could stay a day or two while we prepare our statements to the court."

"Well, of course!" Kasie's father confirmed, finally ending the handshake and offering Dean a hand with the luggage. "Any friend of Kasie's is a friend of ours," her father continued.

The group set off for the car park, luggage in tow. Kasie searched the group for Dee who was suddenly absent from the procession, "Where's Dee gone?" Kasie asked.

"Oh, she took a call," Gwyneth pointed in the direction of the carefree young woman laughing into her phone. At that moment, maybe sensing all eyes on her, Dee turned to see her family and friends waiting on her. She spoke a few final words into the mouthpiece and returned quickly to the group.

"Who was that?" Kasie questioned her as she headed toward the welcoming party.

Dee couldn't wipe the smile off her face, "Marco!" she nearly screamed back at her friend. She softened her voice to a whisper, "He is hopping on a plane right now. He is coming for a mini holiday in Port Douglas."

Dee was literally jumping with joy at the prospect of seeing her lover so soon after she left. "But what about?" Kasie stopped herself from saying his name.

"Apparently," Dee replied, "He is being a miserable tyrant and Marco said he had to leave him before he kills him. His words exactly," she added.

Dean, having heard the entire conversation felt it was his turn to speak. He didn't understand how Kasie could care so much about a man who appeared to show her so little care in return.

"Kasie, why are you so concerned about him, he is a big boy and it will do him the world of good to be without his minder for a while. See how he copes in the big, bad world without him. Besides Marco is a good guy and deserves a break away from that madman. Who knows, Dee here might even persuade him to stay."

Dee just smiled and literally leapt forward, almost skipping to the car park. She was overjoyed to be seeing Marco again. She hadn't wanted to let on to her friend given that she had so much going on herself but she wondered if she was starting to carve out some very real feelings for Coral Cove's second most eligible bachelor. She couldn't wait to show Marco around her little town. She was dying to introduce him to her mother. She would look forward to hearing her mother's honest and open assessment of her friend. She wasn't quite sure at the moment, if it was anything more than friendship, but him deciding to follow her to Australia was definitely a very positive sign that something more serious might be brewing.

The car ride from Cairns to Port Douglas was as always, breathtaking. Kasie was glad to be home, to feel safe and well and re-energised again. She looked toward her two friends, one her best friend for over two decades, the other her new friend from the conservation world. She glanced toward her family and she felt that feeling once more, that lovely, warm feeling of being home.

Dee was a nervous wreck counting down the short time until Marco arrived in Australia. He had told her he needed to travel through Sydney to take a look at an investment there before heading to Port Douglas. Dee spent the majority of her time looking for accommodation and thinking up touristy activities to do with Marco on his short stay.

That left Kasie and Dean alone to hit the beaches during the day and enjoy family dinners at night getting reacquainted with her family.

"So, Dean?" Kasie's Dad started in one night over dinner, "You're not married? No kids?"

"No, have never been married," was his polite response to the father's rather personal line of questioning.

"Do you want to have kids one day?" her father continued.

"Dad!" Kasie yelled at him, "I know what you are doing, please stop! Dean and I are just friends."

Dean looked at Kasie longingly across the table, "Just friends for the time being," he added hopefully.

"Oh?" Kasie's mum added with more than a hint of hopefulness to her tone.

* * *

Having spent a few amazing days back home Kasie was once again at the airport and ready to board a plane to Western Australia, promising her parents that she would return for another visit once her part in the court case was over.

Kasie was thankful that she would be leaving before Marco arrived. It wasn't that she didn't want to see her friend, but she wasn't feeling strong enough or clear enough to deal with one of his famous and skilled interrogations just yet.

Kasie kissed her family and her best friend goodbye before heading to Western Australia with Dean. She promised each of them that if she could, she would spend as much quality time with them back home before she made her way back to Coral Cove.

After saying her final goodbyes, Kasie boarded the plane with her trusted colleague. She regretted not having more time to spend with her loved ones but also felt that time was of the essence on the important task her and Dean had in front of them. Having dedicated very little energy on preparing their statements on the flight to Cairns, Kasie and Dean now settled down for some more preparatory work on their flight.

They compared statistics and any known shark deterrents that were friendly on the environment and promised to cause no harm to the marine life. They argued and debated and wore themselves down until they both fell asleep. Kasie rested her head gently on Dean's shoulder and slept soundly.

The plane landed with a jolt, finally waking the two scientists. Kasie upon waking, becoming vaguely aware that she had been sleeping on Dean's shoulder and offered her sincere apologies, "I'm so sorry, I didn't realise." She was embarrassed beyond words with her over familiarity.

"Any time," her gorgeous companion reassured her. "I quite liked it actually." He leant down and kissed her forehead.

Was she just imagining things, being beyond tired and still very emotional? She had the distinct impression that he was flirting with her.

"Dean..." she began, as the plane taxied to the terminal, "I hope you are ok with us being friends. I know that sounds stupid, but I don't want to give you the wrong impression at all."

"Yes, of course. I understand that. I kiss all my sexy, hot marine researcher friends on the forehead like that," he continued reassuringly. "Shame on you for making me feel bad about it."

Kasie laughed. Dean always made her laugh. He knew how to make light out of any awkward situation and that was what she loved most about him- his ability to laugh at himself. There was no ego with this man. Why would there be? He was the perfect specimen of a man. He had the most gorgeous face, long, blonde flowing locks like the mythical Thor himself, and a hard, tanned strong body. On top of it all, a brain most people would die for.

Plus, Dean had a sense of humour and humility that she had rarely experienced in another human being before. Add to that, his dedication to his work, his unwavering passion for the environment, doing whatever he can to make this planet a better place for future generations to enjoy. Kasie imagined what a perfect partner Dean would actually be.

As the doors of the plane opened and the passengers were directed to the appropriate exit point, Kasie felt a sudden onset of anxiety of what she was about to do. She turned toward Dean, "Do you think we could have a night off and just go grab a beer before we hit the books again?" she wondered.

"Of course," Dean assured her. "Let's check in, drop our bags off and find the nearest pub. I may even give you a game of pool," he teased. "That is if you know how to play of course, I wouldn't want to wager good money with a novice, that wouldn't seem fair," he continued to tease her.

"I will bet you and the horse you rode in on," Kasie joked with him.

"You're on!" Dean laughed back with her.

* * *

Kasie and Dean were sinking their second beer and their second game of pool at the nearest bar they could find.

"Best of three," Dean challenged her, as he sunk the final black ball.

"Oh, that is a game changer. That brings the stakes up."

"Well let's review," Dean continued, "You won the first game which meant I bought your next beer, which by the way I was going to do anyway. I won the second, which was a dance to the song of my choosing. Third game and best of three, the stakes are high!" He laughed to himself as he said it.

"Um, what do I want from you?" Kasie teased him as if already suggesting it would be her win. "What do you have that I want when I beat you?" She was toying with him now.

Dean interrupted her thought with a suggestion, "A kiss!" He paused before continuing with the finer details of the competition. "If I win the third game, I would like a kiss." He repeated his wager as if to make sure he was certain of it.

"Dean?" Kasie tried for her best sweet and innocent voice. "That just wouldn't be appropriate between friends."

"But you kissed me before," Dean retorted.

Kasie remember that fateful night, after having seen her lover kiss Tiffany, seeming to reassure her that his playful tryst with Kasie was just a ruse. Feeling hurt and vengeful, Kasie took her revenge on the nearest and most available bait she had. She kissed Dean without warning, having then discarded it as if it had never happened at all.

Kasie was vaguely aware that she hadn't yet explained or apologised for her very out-of-character behaviour that night.

"But…" Kasie tried to find a rational explanation for why his logic wouldn't work for this particular scenario, but she had none. Other than explaining every little unbelievable detail of The List and the abduction, she couldn't think of another way to clear things up with Dean about what had happened that night of the pool party.

Dean interrupted her thoughts, obviously keen to get started on their third game together. "So, what do you want to bet?" Dean demanded of her.

Kasie thought for just a second before she fired back at him, "I want not to kiss you."

Dean feigned hurt by clutching at his heart with his hand. "Ouch, that hurts! Was our first kiss really that bad?"

"I'm sorry, that didn't come out right. I didn't mean…" Kasie struggled to find the right words to make it up to her friend.

Dean laughed, "That's alright. I understood perfectly what you meant. I just wanted you to feel bad for it."

"Deal." He offered his hand to hers. He wanted for Kasie to begin to believe that there might be alternatives out there to her boss but at the same time he didn't want to push her if her mind was made up. He held hope that she would come to the conclusion herself, yet he couldn't resist the chance to get close to this gorgeous woman again.

"Deal!" She grabbed his hand and shook it. She knew she was playing with fire. She didn't want to risk anything with her boss but she also knew that this man standing before her was kind, considerate and made her feel so comfortable when he was around.

The game began and it was intense, two well-practiced players fighting it out for the title. Kasie being the loser from the previous game, had to break. She got the small balls. Dean was on large. Kasie, with skill and precision was feeling confident, on her next round sinking another two. Dean, not used to losing, sunk three. Kasie began to feel anxious. The pool stick, slightly damp from the moisture of her sweaty palms, slipped from her hands hitting the black ball and sinking it in the nearest hole. The game was over.

"You did that on purpose," Dean laughed. "You finished the game as fast as you could, just to kiss me," he laughed at her.

Having suddenly realised the repercussions of her actions, Kasie was quick to defend her clumsiness, "It just slipped, I missed the ball and it just slipped and hit the black ball."

"I know Kasie," Dean smiled at her. "I am not holding you to that bet. I know it was an accident. Let's play again." He was a gracious victor and could see the sudden panic rise in Kasie as she realised the full ramifications of her loss.

Kasie was taken aback by the ease with which the two of them joked. She admired Dean for not holding her to her promise. Thinking briefly of her boss, she could only imagine how differently he would have responded if she lost to him. He would have probably thrown down his pool stick and wedged her firmly between him and the table, and kissed her passionately on the mouth.

His hands would probably find any excuse to touch her and explore her body. Her mind wandered as she remembered his touch, the passion, as her lips would then meet his in urgency. Her hands grasping at his body, lifting his clothes away. Finding his hot skin.

"Kasie!" Dean yelled a little louder in an attempt to break through to her in her daydream. "It's your break again, seeing as you were the loser, yet again," he joked easily with her. He was enjoying the fun that came with teasing his new friend and especially enjoyed being on their own for the first time. No interruptions, no Dee, no demanding boss.

"No," Kasie corrected him. "Fair is fair, it was my loss and I will pay up." She marched toward Dean and without saying another word, pressed her lips against his. Dean allowed her to continue for just a moment before stopping her.

"No, Kasie," he corrected her. "It was my kiss this time… remember" He looked her in the eye and asked politely. "Are you ready?"

Kasie swallowed hard and replied, "Yes, ready when you are." She didn't know why she was feeling so very nervous.

Dean kissed her, his soft mouth on hers, very gently he traced her lips with his, touching and teasing her with gentle caresses. He kept his hands in place on her hips, as did she on his. She responded with a gentle touch of her own, enjoying the newness of the touch from this sweet, kind man. The kiss ended and both friends stood silent and still as they looked at each other for any clue as to what they should say next.

It didn't take long and Dean was the first to break the tension, "Another beer?" he suggested.

"Yes please!" Kasie replied, grateful that Dean was gentlemanly enough to make the experience as comfortable and contained as possible.

She watched her friend turn and walk confidently toward the bar. She suddenly felt very guilty. A new awareness came to her. She missed him, her lover. Her heart tugged at the thought of him. She tried to gauge how she was feeling after the kiss and she felt shame. A regret that she had treated her new friend so poorly, using him to firstly make her boss jealous at the pool party and then now again allowing him to kiss her in an experiment of sorts to test out any potential feelings for him. She needed to start to put things right and take control of the situation. She pulled her phone out of her pocket and sent a quick text message to her lover:

Hey, sorry if it is late, I just wanted to let you know that I miss you and I am looking forward to coming home soon! Xx

Dean returned from the bar to find Kasie, as she stared at her phone tears had begun to well in her eyes.

"Are you ok, Kasie? What has happened?"

"No, I'm all good." She searched Dean's face attempting to reassure him. "No, really, everything is good," she repeated. She felt a relief that she had finally made the decision once and for all to commit to a future with the man she had left back home in Coral Cove. The man who wanted nothing more than to make her his wife.

With his natural good hearted humour, Dean attempted to once again lighten the mood. "Am I that bad a kisser?" he asked her playfully.

Kasie laughed with him, "No, not at all. It's just," she paused. "If I met you even a few weeks ago this could have all been so different."

Dean looked into her sad face and with all seriousness added, "You know it still can be."

"I'm just not sure Dean. I'm not one hundred percent sure of anything much at the moment."

"Do you really love him Kasie?" Dean asked her gently. He could no longer avoid the obvious emotions Kasie had for her employer. He didn't want to imagine it possible. That a man who he had so little time and respect for, had won the heart of the woman he himself had begun to grow very real feelings for. He hoped that she would say no. That she didn't love her employer, but Dean knew in his heart what the answer to his important question would be.

"I think so." She paused before correcting herself, "Well, I had thought so."

"Which one is it?" He continued to pry for the honest truth from his friend. He sensed a moment of hesitation and wanted to explore that with her. If there was any chance she had doubts about her feelings for her dark-haired boss, he wanted to use that opportunity as the time to tell her how he was beginning to feel about her.

"I don't know at the moment. I mean, I want to. I think I do. Yes, I do. I guess I don't know at the moment how he feels."

He couldn't stop himself from asking the question burning in his mind. "And me? Did I ever stand even the slightest chance?" he pleaded with her.

Kasie looked up at the gorgeous blonde for the first time. "Oh my god, Dean, you couldn't imagine. I wonder even if we were meant… meant to be soul mates?" She paused before adding, "Being with you is just so easy. And being with you is just so much fun. I have loved every second we have been together," she added for reassurance.

"That's all I need Kasie. Just to know that I am still in with a chance. I am happy with that." He laughed again to lighten the deep and meaningful conversation that had come out of nowhere.

* * *

The following day the hard work had begun again. The pair collaborated together with the other researchers and scientists gathered from around the globe to put together the best possible defense against the government's shark legislation. Kasie and Dean worked tirelessly around the clock, reading the various research findings the team had put together. The Government's plan to cull the shark numbers off the coastline made no sense to any of them. They knew of safer and more effective ways of deterring the sharks from the beaches without the killing of any of the beloved creatures.

Sitting back in Dean's hotel room late one night, having spent the last ten hours of the day reading and discussing their various findings, Kasie had a brilliant realisation.

"Do you know what this case really needs?" Kasie asked him. "This really needs some wealthy contributors to donate to the cause. We would need enough money at least to allow some of the team to stay to continue to fight. It would also ensure the consistency in the collection of the research findings, which would assist in the preparation of the arguments against the legislation."

Dean loved the passion of his friend and felt now might be the best time to confess his recent communications from Coral Cove with her. "You know what Kasie? Actually, I think the conservation society may have found their wealthy contributor."

"Really? That is wonderful news, when did this happen? Who and how much?" she probed for further information.

"Who? Well he is a foreign interested party actually and I believe it was a sizeable donation."

"Oh my god Dean, that is amazing, why didn't you tell me earlier? How long have you known this? This is the most wonderful news. We are sure to win the case now." Kasie was overwhelmed. She had become so invested in this fight in her homeland that she couldn't bear the idea of leaving for her adopted country without a clear and committed plan to continue the battle. She knew that with enough money they could keep this fight in the courtroom until they won and the government would be forced to listen to their ideas for a safer ocean for everyone, including the sharks that were the target of their destructive cull.

"Yeah, well I didn't know when I should tell you Kasie. I wasn't sure what the right thing to do was, until now that you mentioned it as an idea, of course."

Kasie felt confused, unsure why Dean wouldn't share this wonderful news with her the moment he heard it himself. "Why are you being so secretive?" She demanded an explanation from him.

"Well I wanted to tell you about the donation before I showed it to anyone else. Just to make sure you were happy enough to allow it to happen."

Kasie was starting to get an uncomfortable feeling in her stomach. "Oh Dean, you are not telling me…" Her voice trailed off. She didn't need to hear any more. She had guessed at Dean's reluctance and had begun to realise why he might have kept it from her. There is only one person she knew who would have the money to get involved in such a large way. Her joy was replaced with a sense of caution at what she might learn next. She understood her lover's passion for ocean conservation but also imagined that a donation would have more to do with Kasie's involvement than she felt comfortable to admit.

"No, Kasie, it's all good, really good actually. I just wanted to show you first." Dean stood and walked to the small desk in the corner of his hotel room. He reached down to hit the power button on his slim, silver laptop. He motioned for Kasie to join him at the desk.

Kasie walked toward him and sat down in front of the screen. Seeing the email open in front of her she began to read,

Dean,

I don't know how to start this email to you except to say that I need to apologise for my behaviour. My actions and my attitude towards you were unforgiveable and I only hope that one day we will meet again, so I can shake your hand, and apologise for my incomprehensible rudeness in person.

If I was able to put into words, an explanation for my despicable behaviour, I could only explain it as this. Imagine that the family you had loved in your lifetime so far had been prematurely ripped from your world. You focused solely on your life's mission, unrelenting in your purpose and pursuit until one day this amazing woman walks into your life and shakes you from your safe and secure little world. No sooner had you professed your love for her (which by the way took me three years to get the courage to do) before she too was stolen from you, not once but twice.

I had only returned her to her life in Coral Cove, when you arrived. Appearing to be there simply to unsettle my world once again. I now realise that you found a soul mate in Kasie. A true friend and passionate ocean lover. I am sorry that I didn't realise this earlier and welcome you into our island family and into our lives.

I am not sure what my future holds. I only hope that Kasie can somehow forgive me for my behaviour, for my jealousy and control. If not and if you and her are able to find true happiness, I wish you nothing but a wonderful life together. Please take care of our adventurous Aussie girl.

I am not asking for your forgiveness. I don't deserve that, but instead I am wanting to show my support for your work and the important case you have travelled to Australia for. I hope you accept my donation to your cause. I am not doing this in the hope that you will share this with Kasie. This is about me trying to fight for our marine life and believing that you are the right person to make a difference.

Yours sincerely,
Just call me... An Anonymous Donor.

Kasie looked up from the screen, tears in her eyes. Dean, having returned to her side now placed a friendly hand on her shoulder. "Kasie, are you ok? I didn't show you to upset you."

"I know Dean," Kasie agreed. "When did he send it?"

"Actually, I received it when we landed in Australia.

Kasie cried quietly. She stood from the table and walked back to the couch. She was touched by the words before her. She was moved to feel the depth of his love for her. His reasoning explained more than just his recent poor behaviour toward Dean. It also explained his jealousy, his control over her and everything around her. She understood now fully his very real fear of losing her, or how he thought he had.

"Kasie," Dean continued, "There is one more thing I feel that I need to tell you."

"Go ahead." She wept not really wanting to hear any more right now but needing to know at the same time. She wasn't sure how much she could manage right now.

Dean moved toward his distressed friend and sat beside her on the couch. "Kasie…" he began, "his donation to the cause was for twenty million dollars."

TWENTY

THE HOUSE

Kasie and Dean worked for much longer than they had imagined. Days had now passed and they were ready to present their material to the courts. Kasie remembered the text message from the previous week, letting her boss know that she was thinking of him. Saying that she missed him and couldn't wait to return to her adopted home. She now remembered again that she hadn't heard back from him. She checked her phone once more to confirm. She thought for a second maybe that she just may have been too busy with the court case to notice his reply.

She did a quick check and confirmed her fear. He hadn't replied back to her message.

Kasie wasn't sure what she should do next. She did a quick calculation and worked out that this two-week absence was the longest time she had gone without speaking to or hearing some word of him in the last three years. Feeling uncertain, but knowing she had to do something, she sent him another text:

Hi there, hope you are still talking to me?
I am looking forward to coming home soon.

I hope I get to see you then? ☺ *xx*

She waited for her reply. It didn't come. Kasie's mind was now racing with reasons why he might be choosing to ignore her. Her thoughts immediately turned to Tiffany. She wondered if there was any chance that Tiffany, playing the role of the concerned friend again had somehow monopolised his attention.

A knock on her hotel room door distracted Kasie from her thoughts. She rose and made her way to greet her visitor. She opened the door to find Dean, standing in front of her, dressed in a crisp white shirt and freshly pressed business pants. "Good morning gorgeous, all ready for our big day?" he asked with excitement.

"As ready as I will ever be," she replied. Grabbing her satchel from the nearby table, she headed back to the door, closing it behind her.

The court case proceeded as they had hoped, in thanks mostly to the huge donation from their loyal friend, which meant that the society was now confident they could be there for the long haul for a drawn-out battle if it came to that. The court had ruled for a temporary injunction to the culling of the sharks off the beaches of Western Australia until further research submitted to the court could be considered.

Kasie was pleased that she had played her role in the successful ruling. She was keen to leave Western Australia and make her way back to her family in Northern Queensland for a visit home. She was acutely aware that she hadn't heard back from her lover and was feeling as if she needed to be around family now as she started to plan her future.

Saying goodbye to her new friend, Dean was going to be difficult. They had spent weeks together, day after day from early in the morning until late at night. She had truly found a soul mate in Dean. A person who was her equal and her idol all wrapped up into one gorgeous body. As much as Kasie wanted to return home to her family, she didn't look forward to fare welling her stunning new friend

Kasie checked out of her hotel room and walked toward the hotel foyer. Dean was there as she had predicted, waiting for her. He was staying behind to continue the work for a while longer. Secretly though, he and a few loyal protestors were planning on taking the hooks down immediately. He had wanted to get more hands-on in this battle for the sharks and he couldn't wait to get on his board and remove the baited hooks for himself. He knew he risked arrest for his actions, but he simply didn't care.

Kasie wished she could stay to help but knew that she had to return to her island paradise soon to continue on her own important conservation work. She did love the idea of sticking it to the government and grabbing a board to paddle out to the drum lines to remove them. She imagined she might see Dean and his co-conspirators in the news, hands tied behind their back being escorted to a police van, still wearing their damp wetsuits. She laughed at the image of it.

She approached Dean in the crowded lobby of the hotel.

"Good morning gorgeous," he greeted her. "How did you sleep?"

"Not well," she admitted as she reached him and leaned toward him to kiss him on the cheek.

"Still no word from him then?" he asked with genuine concern for his friend.

"No, nothing," she confessed.

"Don't worry Kasie, gorgeous. He will message you. He must just be giving you time," Dean assured her. "Do you want me to speak to him?" he asked her, hoping that there might be something he could do to help his friend. "I could ring to say thank you for the donation and find out what he is currently planning for your return?" he offered.

"No. Thanks Dean, you have done so much already." She leant forward and kissed him on the cheek once more. She knew she needed to handle this herself. She was the one after all that left Coral Cove after their disagreement, refusing to see him again face to face until her return.

"When will I see you again?" She turned once more to the smiling blonde surf god in front of her.

"Anytime, gorgeous. We can skype!" he laughed. "And remember, you promised me a surf, so whether it is here, there or Hawaii, we will surf together, and soon!"

"Thanks Dean, you are amazing. I am so glad you walked into my life."

"Love you gorgeous."

"Love you too sexy," she flirted back. The ease that she felt with Dean made her feel comfortable enough to have a little fun with him, knowing that he wouldn't read any more into her jesting than was meant.

Dean watched sadly as Kasie walked to the taxi. "Kasie?" he stopped her as he raced to her side to say one last goodbye. He wrapped his arms around her. "Kasie, please promise me, if he ever does anything to hurt you in any way, you ring me straight away… ok?"

Her friend's care for her brought a smile to her face. "Yes Dean, I promise."

"And…" Dean continued, "And, if you ever change your mind… I will be waiting."

Kasie leant up and kissed her friend on the lips. "You are an incredible man. You won't be single for long. I promise you that."

"An incredible man? If I was that Kasie, you wouldn't be leaving me."

Kasie couldn't argue with his logic. Instead she just hugged him back one last time before stepping into the taxi.

***

Kasie was aboard the plane and worrying about the lack of reply from her boss. She wondered when she would see him again. She looked once more at her messages and checked to see if he had replied. Trying not to concoct a list of plausible reasons behind his silence, she instead closed her eyes and attempted to fall asleep.

Woken by the jolt of the plane's massive tyres hitting the runway of Cairns airport, Kasie glanced out of the window to the familiar sight of home. She was quick to disembark the plane and head straight to the luggage carousel. As she searched for the sign to distinguish her luggage on the carousel, she was jumped from behind by a very excited and very loud Dee.

"You've returned!" Dee giggled as she launched onto her friend's back.

Turning around, Kasie grabbed Dee mid jump and held her tightly in her arms.

"Oh Dee," Kasie began to feel emotional at the sight of the familiar and knowing face. She felt tears behind her eyes. She knew she wasn't doing a very good job at hiding her pain from her friend.

Dee stopped in her tracks. "Kasie, are you ok? What's wrong?"

"No," Kasie replied back. "He isn't talking to me. He won't reply." She began to sob into her friend's arms. "I don't know how I can… what I can say to him to make him understand. He won't reply to me."

"Come on Kasie," Dee comforted her. "You look like you need some rest. You are probably tired and emotional. Don't worry. It will all be ok. You will hear from him soon enough."

Dee looked toward Marco for support and motioned for him to assist their friend.

"Kasie." She heard a comforting male voice speak her name. She looked up and saw his beautiful, smiling face.

"Oh Marco," she yelled as she jumped into his arms. "Marco, you are still here!" She hugged him tightly, finding safety in his warm embrace. She looked around and noticed the absence of her parents. "Is it only you two?" Kasie asked, expecting her parents to be there to greet her again.

"Sorry, only us," Dee added with more than a hint of sarcasm. She knew that Kasie had expected her parents but also knew they were busy with plans of their own.

"Sorry Dee. You know why I asked, an airport pick-up is like a special treat for our parents. I just assumed they would be here."

"Yeah, you are stuck with me and my ugly partner." She tilted her head toward the smiling Marco.

"Kasie, let's get you home," Marco instructed.

"Which one, home or home, home?" Kasie questioned him.

"Either or neither," Marco replied.

"You are a poet and didn't know it," Dee laughed. She seemed to find lots to be happy about lately.

Marco drove the rented open top four-wheel drive from Cairns to Port Douglas. Kasie was surprised at how comfortable it felt to have Marco in her hometown. She watched her two friends laugh and giggle with each other in the front seat. She wondered what was going on with their one remaining friend left home alone.

"How is he?" She was hesitant to say the words out loud to Marco.

Marco responded quickly, and playfully to her, "Who?"

"You know who," Kasie demanded.

"Oh him? He is fine, doing well."

"Yeah… really well from what I understand," Dee added, teasing her friend with the limited information and the innuendos.

"Oh," Kasie tried to find a polite and appropriate response, "That's nice."

Dee and Marco looked at each other and laughed, their hair blowing as the convertible swerved left to right to manipulate the long, winding road from Cairns to Port Douglas.

Kasie looked toward the beautiful, familiar sight of the ocean spread out for miles edging the long road home. It was a comforting view, a surreal scene which could almost have been from a movie set. The view of her hometown was a precious reality. If her own life was depicted in film, this vision before her would have to feature. This winding stretch of road from Cairns to Port Douglas, ascending in parts to reach for the blue skies above before retreating back to meet the white sands or the rocky shoreline. The turquoise waters following her journey beside her rhythmically welcoming her return with splashes of white foam forming with each new roll of the wave.

At times it was as if the sea knew her better than she knew herself. Every delightful memory, overwhelming joy and heartbreaking pain shared with the very waters before her. This was her life, the ocean. It was here she came to re-energise her soul. The warm waters healing wounds, drying tears and comforting her body in its liquid embrace. She suddenly longed to jump in. To let the familiar ocean take away her pain once more.

She felt like a wet blanket, a miserable, energy draining third wheel in the company of her two very joyful and cheery friends. She felt tired and had sweet visions of walking back into her parents' house, taking a long shower and then crawling under the covers for an afternoon nap huddled under the duvet.

She stopped and thought about how miserable she was feeling. She didn't even want to be around herself at the moment. Not normally being a negative person, she tried to lift her mood by picturing a couple of days back home before flying back to Coral Cove. She loved seeing her family and was hoping she might find some time to catch up on the gossip with her old friends. A trip out to the reef would be a nice way to relax and spend time with loved ones, she imagined.

Dee broke through Kasie's now pleasant thoughts, "Oh, and we have to go to a late lunch at Mum's house now. Your parents are already there waiting for you and my Mum has found a special new friend she would like you to meet."

Kasie was quick to respond, "Oh no way Dee, I am in no way interested in anyone your mum wants to set me up with."

"Well I think she would have liked him for me actually, but you know what with this one and all, I didn't really need a fix up." Dee laughed as she teased Marco with her eyes.

"Oh, and I do need a set-up… from your Mum? Dee please, I honestly couldn't think of anything worse to do right now. I am tired and I just need to sleep."

"Sorry Kasie, if you want to cancel lunch with my mum you have to ring and tell her yourself. No way am I going to upset her today. I have never seen her so excited about a potential set-up as she is right now. She seems very confident that she has it right this time."

Kasie sat back in her seat in a huff. It was proving hard today to get past her negative thoughts. Firstly, she was upset about not getting replies from her boss at all and now this ridiculous set-up. She was feeling even more exhausted at hearing Dee's news. All she wanted to do was to be alone. Or better still, grab a boat and head for a snorkel out on the reef. She wondered how long this blind date lunch would take and if there was any chance of a quick swim late this afternoon, just to grab some time alone with her thoughts.

The four-wheel drive steered its way into the little town of Port Douglas, past the main street bustling with locals and tourists. Kasie loved the smell and the sights of her hometown. She loved the water surrounding it on all sides. She loved the cute family owned boutiques, the old-fashioned Queenslander styled hotels and the trendy little bars and restaurants.

She enjoyed watching the busyness of the pier, boats coming and going all day taking tourists to the outer reef for day trips or small charters, hired for a few hours of deep-sea fishing. Kasie watched as the small town now fell behind her and they made the slight ascent to Dee's mother's house on the hill.

Pulling up outside Gwyneth's, Kasie was surprised that no one was rushing out to greet them. It was very unlike her parents and Gwyneth to not rush out to meet their guests, especially their daughters who had both been quite neglectful of their parents' emotional needs of late.

They were always nearly trampling them to death in the mad rush to get to their guests first. Kasie smelt the aroma of meat being charred on the barbeque. With no plans to partake of the meaty banquet herself, she could be assured that Gwyneth and her mother would have prepared something appropriately vegan for her and Dee.

As she got out of the car and walked to the door, Kasie again felt like a third wheel next to Dee and the handsome, Marco. Kasie wondered what Gwyneth thought of Marco and was curious as to how much Dee had shared about why he might have chosen to make an impromptu visit to Port Douglas. As they approached the house, Dee pushed open the front door and ran inside like an excited schoolgirl ready for the introductions to begin.

Gwyneth's flirty laughter was heard well above the rest of the assorted cast. Kasie remembered her friend's warning from earlier. A male guest, a blind date from the thoughtful Gwyneth. She could make out a faint male voice, a dull noise below the overbearing and demanding voices of their three parents who were no doubt at this present moment interrogating the poor victim.

Kasie wondered where Gwyneth may have sourced her latest offering from. She had been doing this for years, bringing home random single men for Dee or Kasie to settle down with. She was all too keen for her daughter to marry and provide her with grandchildren to fill her enormous home. It looked like the tables had turned and today Kasie was the target of her very well-meaning intentions.

Dee had made it to the kitchen. "She's here!" Kasie heard her announce to the room. She made a mental note to seek revenge for her friend's encouragement of this ridiculous set-up later. Kasie paused in the lounge room, trying to feel enthusiastic but not sure if she had the energy to go ahead and walk the few extra steps to the kitchen entrance.

With her inbuilt radar detecting the reluctant guest in the next room, Gwyneth raced through the kitchen entrance and into the lounge in search of Kasie. "Come on, come on! I have someone for you to meet," she encouraged her. She lowered her voice for a moment before adding, "And I think you will like this one. He is very handsome!" She grabbed Kasie by the arm and dragged her to join the others in the kitchen.

Kasie couldn't bear to look up, as unceremoniously she was tossed into the centre of the room, all eyes on her as Gwyneth announced to the hungry crowd, "This is her, the one I told you about. This is Kasie."

Her introductions continued, "And Kasie, this is… " Kasie had no choice now but to look up and find the face of the surprise male guest, her supposed blind date, in the room with her. She looked up at the tall, handsome dark-haired man with the stunning emerald eyes and was quick to interrupt Gwyneth.

"We've met before."

The sexy man in front of her politely offered his hand to her. "Hi Kase," he whispered in his sexy soft voice. "It's nice to see you again."

Dee and Marco broke into raucous laughter like two giddy teenagers.

Gwyneth, quickly realising that a prank had been played, began demanding answers of her daughter and Marco. "What's this about? You knew he knew her? Why didn't you say something? You've made me look like a fool."

Kasie was the one to answer. She watched her friends, doubled over in laughter. She wanted to relieve the lovely Gwyneth of her curiosity. "We met while I was in Coral Cove. We actually work together… kind of." Kasie paused as she smiled at the familiar face of her lover, "Actually, he is my boss."

"Oh," Gwyneth replied with some confusion. She turned to the handsome new guest, "But when you said you had come to Port Douglas to give Marco a lift, I assumed you were from Queensland somewhere."

Dee cleared up the confusion, "Well you know what they say about assuming, Mother." Dee continued to laugh with Marco.

Kasie couldn't help but see the humour in the situation and the very logical reason Gwyneth would have assumed her guest was picking his friend up in a car instead of a private jet.

"So, that is why you are here?" Kasie was a little disappointed to realise that her friend wasn't here to see her but instead here to pick up Marco and return him home.

He leant forward and whispered so the others couldn't hear, "I have a spare seat if you would like to come home with me."

Kasie loved hearing that word fall from his mouth once more. Home, she thought to herself. She smiled at her gorgeous lover. She was relieved to see him standing there in front of her and acting like he had forgiven her for her unexpected and unpleasant departure from the mansion on their last meeting.

Kasie's mother interrupted the merriment and the secret whisperings between the friends, "How about we eat then?"

Sitting around the table, Dee and Marco side by side, barely able to contain themselves, Kasie and her boss sat opposite each other sharing secret glances when the others weren't watching them. The parents, with years of practice under their belt, continued to fire questions at the four young friends.

"When do you think you will return home, Marco?"

Marco looked toward his boss, as if for confirmation of their departure date and time. "Day after tomorrow, I believe," he finally responded.

Kasie added her updated news as well, "So am I actually, I am going to travel home with the boys."

"Home?" her mother questioned her with a critical tone. "This is your home, Kasie and I didn't imagine you would be leaving this quickly. You just got here."

Dee was the next to speak, "And actually, if there is one more spare seat in the…" she paused for the right word, "transport, I was hoping to join you all." She looked toward the tall bachelor for approval to catch a lift.

Without hearing his reply, Gwyneth interrupted, "But Dee you just got back. Don't you think you need to return to work? They had been kind enough to give you this impromptu little holiday. I think you need to let them know you will be returning soon."

"Actually Mum, I am resigning. I have been offered some work in Coral Cove. A really great opportunity to work in a new position that has just become vacant in the tourism industry."

Kasie couldn't contain her excitement, much to the displeasure of Gwyneth and her parents. She jumped up and hugged her best friend. The girls stood for a moment beside the dining table, squeezing each other tight. Both feeling so very happy and relieved that they would be living together once more. Kasie was beyond elated at the exciting news. She could hardly believe what she was hearing. This was like a dream come true for her.

Kasie's dad spoke first, "You know what Dee will say next, I'll be gone for just a year."

Kasie's mum added the finishing touch to their well-oiled script, "And then they are gone for three years… three years." She added the final two words for a dramatic effect.

Their boss spoke up, "Well actually. It might not be necessary for Kasie and Dee to stay away that long at all."

Dee and Kasie looked strangely at their friend, not quite understanding what he meant by his vague comment to their parents.

He continued his explanation, "Kasie has told me about a lovely little beach not far from here, Oaks Beach. I have seen a house for sale there and I thought if the company I work for bought a house there both of the girls could return home for a visit more often, and Marco of course, if he chose to. We could use it as a second base as we look towards expanding our conservation efforts further afield. Coral Cove would of course remain our head office, but Oaks Beach looks like the perfect place for an expansion to our organisation."

Kasie smiled at her boss. She knew exactly what he was doing. She knew about his sudden interest in the fight for the sharks in Australia. She understood that there would be no reason for him to set up a workspace here. She knew he was just making an excuse for her to be able to continue to do the work she loved and stay in closer contact with her parents.

"Well that is a lovely thought young man," Gwyneth responded. "But those houses on Oaks Beach, they are not cheap. They might be a little out of your price range, but it is a very lovely thought, nevertheless."

Dee nearly spat out her food at her mother's latest assumption. Marco smirked without saying a word. Kasie looked at her friends and couldn't help but form a huge smile on her face.

Gwyneth, sensing she was the butt of the joke for the second time that day demanded an explanation from her daughter. "What now?" she nearly yelled at her.

"It's nothing," Dee managed to say as she continued to laugh behind her hand. None of the friends thought it necessary to share the extent of the new guest's vast fortune.

* * *

The next morning the four friends jumped back into the four-wheel drive and made their way the short distance to Oaks Beach. Having seen the house and fallen madly in love with it, appropriate arrangements were made for the contract to be written up. Kasie had dreamt of owning a house on Oaks Beach from the day she first found the small oasis. She stood in awe, staring at the remarkable three-storey home that her boss had just purchased.

She remembered back to the first time she had stumbled across the hidden gem that was Oaks Beach. The gorgeous little beach was tucked away with just a few privately owned houses lining the white, sandy shore. On that day, years ago, she had sat on the beach and glanced back at one of the huge homes set right on the edge of the sand.

She fell instantly in love with the beach and she daydreamed as she looked at the long rope and wood swing that someone had made and imagined her children one day playing on the large tree that housed it.

She had imagined Oaks Beach could be the perfect outdoor upbringing her children would relish if they lived here. She secretly made a promise to herself, having only later ever shared it with just one person, that if she could ever afford it, she would one day return to the beach and buy that very house.

Her gorgeous lover broke through her warm memory. His tone was hopeful and thoughtful, "Do you think your parents will be happy to visit their grandchildren here one day?"

She ignored his seemingly innocent question, seeing it as his way of letting her know in no uncertain terms, why he purchased the house, as if she didn't have enough of a clue already.

He made it all look so easy. Moving around the world as he pleased in his own private jet, buying properties, business, boats whenever he needed without ever having to think of how he might afford it. She imagined it must be comforting to have that much money. She turned to her friend, to share her reflection and test out her latest theory.

"Is it a good thing having all your money?" she asked him.

He gave it a thoughtful moment before answering. "Sometimes," he answered. "Right now, it feels a good thing because I am able to share it with the people I love. Other times, it feels like a burden." He paused as the thought continued to turn in his head. "I am hoping that one day in the very near future, I will have a wife to help me with my burden." He smiled his gorgeous, perfect smile at Kasie.

"Lucky girl," she smirked as if to brush off the innuendo that it might be her, he was referring to.

"No… lucky me!" he corrected her.

Sensing this was the perfect opportunity to find out from Kasie what the current state of their complicated relationship was, he dared to ask her the question he guessed she had been dreading. He glanced quickly over his shoulder first to make sure their two friends were far enough out of earshot to hear their personal discussion. He collected the courage to speak the words.

"Kase, what happens with us now?"

Kasie had thought about this on the plane flight back to Cairns and probably long before that in those moments when she was brave enough to allow herself to daydream that they would be together once more.

"I actually had a thought," Kasie answered him with a cheerful and hopeful tone to her voice.

"Do tell?" He was secretly dying to hear her idea. Hoping that it somehow involved her moving into the mansion, accepting a marriage proposal and planning a future together.

"I thought that you could take me on a date when we get home," Kasie shared her plan.

He paused, not expecting the idea Kasie had proposed but thankful that it was at least heading in the same direction as his previous planning. "A date?" His tone was playful. "And what does that involve? A sleepover I hope?"

"No, definitely no sleepovers on the first date. What sort of girl do you think I am?" Kasie laughed with him, flirting just a little.

"What if the date lasted a week?" He found a hopeful loophole to her plan.

"No, no sleepovers! A date could be you picking me up from my house, dinner, a bottle of nice wine, conversation, getting to know each other all over again," she explained her plan in more detail.

"Sounds like fun," he replied with genuine interest.

"Oh, but there is something I think I should tell you," Kasie continued. She thought now was the best time to be honest with her boss.

"That doesn't sound good," he replied, wondering what more needed to be said. He had hoped it didn't involve mention of Dean but feared he was about to hear his name again.

"It's Dean." Kasie paused, not sure of the reaction she might get to the news she was about to share. She was hesitant to say the next few words out loud but knew that she needed to start this next part of the journey with her lover with all honesty and everything laid out in front of them. "I kissed him."

He was relieved that was all Kasie needed to say. "Yes. I know. I saw you," he reminded her.

"Um," Kasie hesitated once more.

"Oh, I see," was his short response. His downturned face displayed his obvious hurt. He suddenly realised that his greatest fear was quickly becoming a real possibility. "And is there more to tell?"

Kasie was quick to answer this time. "No, it was just one kiss."

Her friend seemed relieved to hear this additional clarification. He edged closer to her again, lowering his voice as he asked her, "Was it as good as our kisses?" He smiled at her, appearing confident that her answer would be a positive one.

Kasie giggled. She wasn't quite sure how to respond to the very forward question. "Let's just say… that a woman doesn't kiss and tell."

"That sounds very non-committal." Her handsome friend continued, "Do you think you need reminding just in case you have forgotten?"

Kasie looked sheepish, "Maybe?" That was all the encouragement she needed to give before her sexy companion leant forward and kissed her once more.

After spending the next day with her family and filling them in with a little more detail on the tall, handsome stranger in their house, Kasie felt ready to say goodbye again. It seemed easier this time than when she left Port Douglas three years ago. Helped in a large way by the fact that she had a home and a new life waiting back there for her.

Kasie was excited that Dee would be returning with her and sharing her house and her life again. Kasie felt as if everything was how it should be. She made a solemn promise that she would return to visit her family more often, and given that the stunning beach house on Oaks Beach lay vacant eagerly awaiting her arrival made it even more appealing to come home regularly.

She guessed that setting up a second base near Port Douglas would be a priority for them all and she relished the opportunity to maybe have her parents involved, even if in some small way.

Kasie's father and mother kissed her goodbye at the airport, still blissfully unaware of the mode of transport the four friends were about to board. Thinking instead it was best for them to find out little by little the details of the man who one day may become their son-in-law, Kasie didn't want to overwhelm them with too much at once.

Gwyneth kissed Dee goodbye, making Marco promise to bring her daughter back for a visit soon. The three parents bid farewell to their young guests. All were still obviously very curious about this tall, mysterious stranger and his best friend who seemed to be stealing their daughters away yet again.

"Come back soon!" all the parents yelled in near unison at their departing daughters.

"And check on the house often," Kasie yelled back to them.

"Oh, we will," Gwyneth replied with an eager smile.

The friends turned around one final time and made their way to the private terminal to board their luxury ride home.

TWENTY-ONE

THE DATE

Having badgered Kasie for most of the flight home to commit to a night and time for their date, Kasie found herself enjoying teasing her lover just a little too much, practically making him beg her for a commitment to the promised date night.

Guessing that this time of flirting and fun and teasing might one day come to an end, she relished the last chance to play with him. Having finally agreed to a Friday night date, she calculated in her head she had only two days to find the perfect dress.

All of the friends returned home to their lives. Dee as promised moved into Kasie's spare room at the house, proving to be a very welcome companion for her on their quiet nights in. Dee immediately started her new job promoting the tourism of the reef in lieu of Eric Cobalt's termination of contract.

Marco picked up where he left off with an even greater sense of wellbeing than he had felt in years. Kasie returned the very next day to her work at the research facility and as promised skyped Dean back in Australia to fill him in on everything that had happened since she left Western Australia.

The next two days were busy, but Kasie managed to find what she thought was the perfect date dress. Friday night came around all too quickly.

As scheduled, he arrived to pick her up from her house for the date and of course, on time to the minute. Kasie heard her friend park the car and walk the few stairs to her front door. She turned to Marco and Dee on her lounge watching a game.

Neither of them appeared bothered to look in her direction as she played nervously with her hair while she stood waiting by the door. She pleaded with them for the tenth time that night, "Are you sure this looks ok?" She yearned for their feedback.

"Just go already Kasie. God the man has seen you naked, I hardly think he is going to care what your new dress looks like," Dee answered before returning her attention back to the television. "And I hardly imagine you will be wearing it for long anyway," she laughed at her own assumption.

"You look beautiful," Marco reassured her. He could see how nervous she was but really didn't understand why after all they had already shared and promised to each other.

Kasie took a deep breath and opened the door just as her handsome date was about to knock. He smiled a knowing smile at her, obviously hearing all of the conversation from behind the closed door, he was quick to speak.

"They are correct." He looked her up and down and licked his lips for effect. "On all accounts, you do look beautiful and yes I have seen you naked." He glanced skyward for a moment closing his eyes at the memory. "And," he continued, his emerald green eyes locked onto hers, "You won't be wearing that dress for very long anyway."

"Stop," she blushed as she pushed him out of the doorway with her palm. "Go." She pointed toward, the car urging him to get back into it.

"Night Dee, Marco," he yelled back at his friends inside the house as Kasie pulled the door shut behind her. "Don't wait up for her."

"Where to?" she asked once outside the house.
"I have made reservations at a very special venue."

"Do tell!" She was beyond curious wanting to know where they were going for their very special first date.

"It's a bit of a drive, hope you don't mind," was all he appeared willing to divulge to her.

"I'm suddenly very nervous," she confessed as she stepped into the car. He held the door open for her and closed it softly behind her once she had found her comfortable seat.

They were unusually quiet on the drive. Kasie was feeling more and more restless as they made their way to the secret location.

She hadn't expected to feel this excited. But it was a nice kind of nervous energy. Anticipating the date, she wondered where they might go, what they might talk about. How formal they would be able to remain with each other. She wondered as well, how long it would take for one of them to lose all control and jump on the other, ripping clothes off as quickly as they could.

She guessed it was fortunate that they had planned a public place for dinner. This at least prevented any lapse in control. The energy between them was electric. She could feel it even without touching or talking. She knew he was on his best behaviour tonight, trying desperately to impress and make this the most romantic first date ever. She only hoped she could show the same control, which up until now, she had at times really struggled with.

Kasie also wondered what this meant now for the status of their relationship. Did this first formal date signal the beginning of the inevitable or were they both still testing each other out? Spending time together to see if this might progress into something more.

Things had happened the wrong way around for Kasie, or at least how she imagined things should progress in relationships. This first date would normally signal the start of an intention to get to know one another better. The beginning of a commitment for something that could possibly resemble a future together. But for the two of them, they had already made that promise of a future together or at least made a declaration to each other of their desire to be together.

The house in Oaks Beach, the declaration of love, the knowledge that a marriage proposal was somewhere in their future made this the most intense first date experience Kasie had ever had. It seemed the only condition that they hadn't officially agreed upon yet was how many children they would like to have together. The thought of it made her want to jump from the moving car. This really was happening all so very quickly and Kasie knew she would have to keep her anxiousness in check. She turned to view her companion.

His wide smile back to her bought with it a sense of ease that he understood that they were both needing some more time to get used to the reality that this was actually happening for them.

Enjoying the quiet, she was surprised that the drive to the location was much shorter than she had expected.

As the car pulled into the vacant space beside the water at the wharf, Kasie wondered if he had purposefully not parked in the undercover parking for fear that it would trigger painful memories for her. She loved that about her friend. That he was always thoughtful with the little details. He would think about how she might feel about situations, places and people and was always very mindful to put her needs first.

He was also interested in her and remembered the little details, the fact that she had shared her love of this hidden little beach called Oaks Beach back home and her dream to one day own a house there. She truly appreciated the fact that he was curious about her, really listened and genuinely seemed to care.

He had made his way to her side of the vehicle, opened her door and offered his hand as she swung her legs around and exited the car. She looked up at the beautiful line of trendy little restaurants on the wharf and wondered which one he was taking her to. She was surprised as they walked silently past each restaurant, looking in she watched the gorgeous, well-dressed Friday night crowds busily chatting and dining away.

They both saw several of their friends and waved their hands in greeting, everyone unfazed by the town's heir out on an obvious date with the new head of his conservation society. They walked past the final bar. Kasie felt more confused than ever, when they began to make their way down the moorings and toward the small tender, tied on neatly at the very end of the walkway.

He stood before her, still not saying a word, before bending down to carefully remove her shoes, first one and then the other. He then placed her gorgeous, sparkly new heels into the boat. He proceeded to turn around and hold out his hand to take hers. Assisting her in to the tender and then hopping in behind her, he immediately reached over grabbing a small soft throw and placed it gently around her to shield her from the cold night air.

He started the motor and made his way carefully out to the reef. She could see the luxury cruiser in the distance, anchored in her favourite position on the reef, the spot where the clear blue water of the reef met the dark blue of the deeper ocean beyond.

From a distance the boat looked like one big flame flickering in front of a backdrop of the perfect black night sky. The moon was just slightly beaming a small amount of light onto the nearing location. As they got closer she could see the hundreds of tea light candles placed with care and thought on every level of the boat, flickering away, signaling to them for safe passage as they awaited their arrival.

As the couple pulled along the stern of the boat, two men rushed out to take the rope from the skilful sailor. One of the men then offered her a hand, while her date placed his palm on the small of her back to guide her. Stepping onto the boat, she turned to watch her friend, her shoes in his hand, lunge forward and onto the cruiser. He held out his hand to take hers.

"I have booked the best table in the house for tonight." He smiled his most gorgeous smile at her.

Her date guided her slowly to the table set out on the second deck of the boat. It offered shelter from the night's breeze and the perfect location to take in the breathtaking view. The sky was clear with barely a cloud visible against the dark blue backdrop. The breeze gentle and warm against her skin tingled with excitement at its breathy light touch. The large vessel swayed ever so gently. The comforting sounds of the calm sea providing just a hint of an incoming tide to supply the movement of the hull against the deep ocean.

He gently placed her shoes down beside the table, before he positioned his strong hands on the back of the chair, pulling it out for his date to take her place on the small table for two. He moved to the opposite side of the tastefully decorated setting and took his seat across from her. The moonlight shone down to illuminate the table. Red rose buds were placed carefully in a delicate vase between them. Crystal glasses reflected the glistening sparkle of the flickering candles on all sides of them.

"This looks absolutely amazing. You are truly a hopeless romantic, aren't you?" Kasie complimented her date.

"Are you impressed?" he asked her. He smiled at her compliment sensing that she was pleased with the efforts he had gone to personally to ensure this date was everything that she had wished for.

"Very much so," she replied.

He felt hopeful. "So, would you say I am on track to get a second date then?" He was keen to begin negotiations for the advancement of their relationship.

Kasie laughed, "Don't get too far ahead of yourself now. We haven't even eaten yet."

For the first time, Kasie noticed the music playing in the background. She smiled at her gorgeous date. "Is that the soundtrack from Titanic?" she asked him. She was surprised that he even remembered watching the movie together. So much seemed to have passed since that time when the two of them were on this very boat alone watching her favourite movie.

"Yes, I hope it isn't a bad omen to play it while we are at sea."

"I am sure we will be fine, especially considering we're at anchor."

"We don't have to be, you know. Just say the word and we can go wherever you like." He was keen to take her away again. As much as he made light of the suggestion, it would only take her quick agreement for him to raise anchor and sail away together to wherever the mood took them.

Before she had a chance to respond to his playful banter, a waiter appeared. He began by first pouring Kasie a glass of champagne before moving to her date and pouring his. The waiter returned to Kasie's side, removing the white linen napkin from its folded position in front of her and placing it gently in her lap.

Moving toward her date, he repeated the well-rehearsed formality. Kasie's eyes didn't leave the stunning man in front of her. Staring intently into his dark green eyes, she felt like she was in a wonderful dream. This was the most perfect first date she could ever have imagined. She continued to stare into his eyes, not speaking, just smiling back at him.

He smiled at her and raised his left eyebrow as his smile somehow widened. He broke from their stare to point with his eyes towards the small back box sitting on the table in front of her. Oblivious to the small, luxurious box a moment earlier she now examined it without touching it.

Having been hidden under the napkin its presence was magically revealed with the precision of the experienced waiter's small action. Her heart did a backflip as she suddenly realised the enormity of what was happening.

"Oh no," she let slip out without thinking about the hurt the words could cause.

He smiled at her, but feigned a disappointed tone, "I hope that isn't your response to a question I haven't yet asked you," he joked with her in an obvious attempt to lighten the mood.

"It's just… it's our first date. I didn't think you would…" she stammered with her words. She couldn't find the right way to explain to him that she simply wasn't ready for a proposal yet.

"I didn't." He relieved her of her anxiety. "I wouldn't do that to you… just yet," he added playfully. "It isn't a ring, Kase, it is just a present. Not that I'm not dying to ask you to marry me, but that probably wouldn't be appropriate behaviour for a first date. Would it now?"

"Open it!" he encouraged her.

Feeling instantly relieved, she picked up the small black box. Opening the box carefully she was suddenly very excited to find out what was inside. She lifted the lid.

"Oh my… oh…" was all she could say. Tears welled in her eyes. Her voice cracked and stumbled, as she was barely able to contain herself at the vision in front of her.

"This is the most gorgeous thing I have ever seen."

He stood from the table as she took the necklace from the box. Placing it in her soft hands, she felt the smooth, even surface of the heart-shaped green glass. She marveled at the intricately detailed gold surrounds and the delicate gold chain that held it.

Making his way to her side he finally spoke, "It is the heart of the ocean. Do you remember?"

"Of course, this is the glass we found on Long Island. Have you had it the whole time?"

"Yes. I had it made into a necklace and was just waiting for the perfect time to give it to you."

"This is the most romantic thing any man has ever done for me," she complimented him.

"Do you like it?" he asked.

"I love it! It is priceless!" she was quick to respond. "I will keep this forever."

She looked at its beauty and uniqueness once more. "My heart of the ocean."

He took the necklace from her hands and placed it around her neck, bending down to give her a gentle kiss on the lips when he had finished. She placed her hand on the warm green surface and savoured the moment.

She couldn't believe he had made this for her. After doubting his romantic side while watching Titanic. She had concerns then as to how compatible they might be. But this, keeping this piece of glass, long after she had forgotten he still had it. Taking the time to create this piece of jewellery. Creating the space and time to present it to her. Kasie was without words. This was the single most romantic thing anyone had done for her.

Their first course arrived only moments later. Still in awe of the beautiful gift she had received her mind was racing with the thought of him, that day placing the precious glass into his back pocket. She wondered if then and there he knew what he was going to do with it.

Trying to focus her attention back to her handsome date, she made a suggestion, "How about we ask each other questions like we would if this was our actual first date."

"It is our first date," he responded.

"Ok, well, like we are just getting to know one another," she corrected herself.

"Ok, I will start. What is your favourite colour?" he began

"Green," she answered immediately, thinking of the gorgeous piece of jewellery around her neck. "Green, the colour of my heart of the ocean," she paused before adding, "Emerald green, like the colour of your sexy eyes."

She laughed at the ease with which the compliment came. "But really," she giggled, "Is that as good as you've got for first date conversation?"

"You are putting me under a lot of pressure tonight. I hope you realise that Kase? Ok, I'll try again." He paused thinking about what question might humour her enough to gain her satisfaction. "How many children should we have together?"

She laughed a nervous laugh at his directness. "Wow, you really went from one extreme to the other there. Is there ever a middle ground with you?" she challenged. She felt so connected to him, knowing she had wondered this exact thing only moments earlier in their car ride here.

"Ok, how about this?" He tried again to pitch the conversation at the right tone. "Where would you like to go on our second date?" He smiled a cheeky grin at her, no longer in any doubt as to their future together.

"Ok, that's a good question, so assuming you actually get a second date," she teased. "When do you think it might be?"

His smiled widened, his deep emerald green eyes staring intently at hers, he parted his mouth ever so slightly before addressing her slowly in his sexy whisper,

"I was thinking… maybe tomorrow… breakfast?"

She laughed at his confidence, his supposed innocent attempt to keep her for the night on the boat, she had guessed. She smiled back at him and with her best flirty, sexy response, whispered to him,

"Maybe"

She felt the skin of her cheeks turn red with the heat rising in her body. She was nervous at the thought of their imminent first night together on his boat, in his cabin. "You are obsessed," she flirted with him.

"I am obsessed Kase. I am obsessed with you. So much so I named her after you. Have you not noticed before now?" He lifted his open palm to proudly point to the shiny silver letters displayed on the wall of the second deck of the massive vessel.

For the first time, Kasie noticed the name of his boat. She had never really taken note before and never would she have known she was the inspiration behind this great honour. She mouthed the name out loud,

"Obsession"

She smiled a huge smile. She was now sure. There was no more doubt in her mind. This was that magical moment she had always hoped for. The man she loved had done something so special for her that her tears welled and her throat got caught and she knew finally and with absolute certainty that he was the one!

WANT TO BE A GUEST CONTRIBUTOR?

Did you notice that our billionaire bachelor didn't have a name? I have a little confession to make… I fell in love.

While writing THE LIST and the second book of the series, THE REEF, I surprised myself when I fell in love with the island prince. I had every intention of disclosing his name when Kasie wrote her note to him at the end of THE LIST. I had planned for her to start her letter with Dear ____.

When it came time to write it, no name seemed worthy of him, so instead I continued on with the THE REEF, never sharing his name. A couple of times, our couple tease us and we think we are going to hear it, but alas, they keep the secret to themselves.

This is where you, my reader, can play an important role. I want to hear from you all, what name you think our billionaire bachelor/conservationist/island prince should be named.

Sign up to kelliemcox.com or any of my social media contacts. Take a photo of yourself with the book THE LIST or THE REEF or both and let me know what you want our bachelor to be named and why. Add the hashtag #kelliemcox

As the name suggestions come through, I will choose my favourites and those readers will be the very first to receive a printed copy of my novel, THE LAST FIRST KISS. A personally signed copy will be sent to you to thank you for your inspiration.

ACKNOWLEDGEMENTS

This publishing journey is shared with family and friends, so that the end result is something I hope we can all feel a part of. I am truly honoured to have you all play an important role in the creation of this book with me.

My children Blair and Connor, you truly are the brains and business behind my books. Blair, you create gorgeous book covers that attract readers. They are drawn to your designs. Your creative and technical support is invaluable. Connor, you make the engine behind the books function. You inspire me and keep me accountable. You both joked about my endless editing, I hope you are finally happy to see the books coming to life.

The talent behind the words, my editor and proofreader, Nadine Meyn. I sometimes think you are more dedicated to the manuscripts than I am. You make me believe your job is easy until I see the final edit and realise you spent much more than just your dedicated hours to clean up my work. I am so fortunate to have you in my life.

ACKNOWLEDGEMENTS

My alpha readers, Mark Simmons and Melissa Spilstead, the two of you constantly keep me busy, writing and re-writing endings and identifying storylines that can be improved with a tweak here and there.

My beta reader on this book, Margaret Cox. You loved this story and wanted to see it in print. Your enthusiasm for THE LIST and THE REEF encouraged me to tell this beautiful love story.

And to Georgina Winters, for gifting me these gorgeous images that became the book covers. They were just beautiful. Thank You!

To my readers. Wow, you all were incredible with your enthusiasm for my debut novel, MURDEROUS INTENT. I have taken all of your feedback on board. For these second and third novels, I have added more sexy bits (at your request) and a romantic ending. I know you all enjoy the feel-good ending.